Malevolent Flesh

By

Drew Forest

Also Available by Drew Forest

The Corpse Rooms

Reading the Palms of Dolls

Published internationally by Drew Forest

© **Drew Forest 2017**

ASIN: B074SYV149
ISBN: 9781522034537
ISBN-10: 1522034536
ISBN-13: 978-1522034537

*

The relationship between a brother and sister lies at the heart of this story and though faced with unusual hardships, there is no denying the bond that inevitably ties them. It would only serve fitting that I would dedicate this book to my very own sister - quite like the characters in this work of fiction, she has been nothing but a supportive force throughout my years on this little orbiting planet.

Mandy, this one is for you.

*

"I think it was when I ran into Kerouac and Burroughs - when I was 17 - that I realised I was talking through an empty skull... I wasn't thinking my own thoughts or saying my own thoughts."

- Allen Ginsberg

Malevolent Flesh - A Stranger Approaches…

…Her thin, bone-white arms began to stretch out towards Tyler, her eyes firmly fixed in his direction. He realised she was pointing directly at him, her wide glassy eyes were pinned open in a look of absolute terror. The man that she was sat with looked on at her in disbelief, it was clear that her response had come from out of the blue. The woman had turned deathly pale and her thin shoulder length hair clung to her perspiring face.

She screamed again and with her finger still pointed, she began to stagger from her side of the restaurant to where Tyler sat. There was no way he could move from his seat, the entire situation had caused him to freeze to the spot, his heart raced with a quick succession of hammer-like thumps and dread descended over the entirety of his body. *Why is this woman screaming and pointing at me? Why is she approaching me?*

No one thought to stop her as she slowly made her way over to his table, her finger still outstretched as though accusing him of some unspoken crime. She was a few feet away when Tyler realised that he should attempt to flee, there was clearly something very wrong about this woman and he could not predict what she was going to do once she had reached him. Her pupils had become small black dots and the whites of her eyes seemed to glow with the essence of something otherworldly. It was something far more sinister than anything he had encountered on this plane of existence. Her mouth appeared to be trembling, it wasn't until she was merely a foot or two away that he realised she was saying something. She spoke faintly, each word was broken up but he could just about make out that she was saying, *"you, it's you…"*

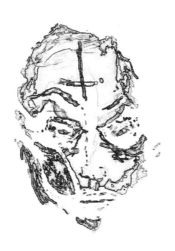

Prologue

Life and death.

The seemingly inevitable mortal transition that could snatch a life within a moment. Sometimes the transition may progress a little longer, or sometimes death chooses to transpire over a considerable amount of time - a stretching departure from this world and this universe as we know it. Yet no one wants a slow death - no one wants to leave their bodies gradually, forced to savour each and every moment knowing that it is their last, like grains of sand lost to the breeze. To pass on whilst asleep, cocooned within the confines of a pleasant dream; the event occurring painlessly and effortlessly may be considered by some as the perfect death.

She had encountered death in its many forms during the course of her life, but not a single one of them had been perfect. In fact, they had been quite far from it.

And it was in that moment - as she witnessed the life depart from the mangled body, that each and every vein in her frail body suddenly became engorged with blood. The hot sticky fluid, reminiscent of some form of organic magma rushed through her arteries with such velocity, that she too, became convinced that she was destined to depart this earth in that very second. And she accepted that terrifying notion - she embraced it with open arms and exhaled with a momentary taste of peace, convinced that it was to be her final breath. Yet, adrenaline coursed through her system ascending her consciousness to a an entirely new level of anxiety. Synapses seemed to crackle and fire, while further chemicals surged through her body and her once-perfect 20/20 vision was suddenly clouded by a cascade of white flecks that resembled surgically structured snow-flakes. She had been temporarily paralysed with the realisation of what had happened. This was the moment she was sure that she was due to pass from her corporeal being and drift into the great beyond.

This was the moment that changed everything.

Life and death.

As quick as flicking a switch.

On - off.

Yet it didn't arrive.

Not for her.

And not this time.

Instead, the silence was pierced with a gut wrenching scream that escaped her lungs with such force that she was sure she would never speak again. What have I done? What have I done? She internally repeated those very same words to herself - over and over. The question joined the expanding cacophony that swirled in her mind within that very moment, blanketed by the maddening realisation of of what had just occurred.

What have I done? She continued, what have I done?

Chapter One

Some days, the dark thoughts were fleeting.

They would visit Tyler in a succession of pin pricks - each one providing a new sinister motive. For the thirty three years of his life, he had developed numerous coping strategies - ways and means to banish the pain that each sharp stab provoked within himself. He'd gotten accustomed to feigning the face of a content man - a man who had his shit together and could brush off the creeping sensation of impending doom whenever it would rear its hideous face. Acquaintances had often described him as *'laid-back'* - a seemingly competent advocate in not being defeated by the challenges that life frequently threw in his direction. He'd bat those challenges out of the park - *'a home run'*, as some of his state-side co-workers would say. He was a winner in the eyes of those that knew him. Except, the truth of the matter was that these people had only been introduced to the carefully refined masked-version of Tyler Hamilton. Before he'd even gotten out of bed and wiped the sleep from his eyes, Tyler would carefully slip the mask on. It had become nothing more than a finely honed instinct.

Mask on.

Face the world.

It was an impenetrable device and had allowed him to sail through a number of different challenges in his life. His father's suicide, his five year battle with cancer, the loss of a number of friends who had voiced their close minded opinions about his lifestyle *'choice'*, the New Years eve party he had drunk himself into a stupor and haphazardly walked into oncoming traffic.

Mask on.

Face the world.

Tyler Hamilton did not consider himself to be a strong person. It was merely the survivalist mentality that possessed his body and mind whenever he donned that perfectly presented mask. Without it, he knew he wouldn't be able to deal with any of the daily challenges that inevitably introduced themselves over the course of the average day. In fact, it was a Thursday in October when he discovered that his strategy was not fool-proof.

It failed him like never before.

He maintained a steady pace as he walked down a street that he had never visited before. Orange and red leaves occasionally fluttered from the tall sycamores like confetti, though there was no cause to celebrate on this particular day. The houses seemed to be lined perfectly and precisely on either side of the empty road presenting the epitome of a typical suburban English street on a midweek afternoon. He inhaled the cool autumnal air as he dissected the conversation that had taken place a few hours earlier.

"Tyler, you know this pains me to say and we've put everything in place to retain as many of our dedicated staff members on the team. The voluntary redundancy plan just did not work, so we've had to look at other ways of keeping the business afloat. Unfortunately, and as you are fully aware, you haven't been reaching target figures for a few months now. I'm so sorry to have to tell you this Tyler, I really am, but we have to let you go, effective immediately."

Tyler's eyes had remained fixated on the mouth of his boss as he spoke those shell-less words. His chapped lips appeared to perfectly frame each syllable as they succinctly popped from his vocal chords. His articulation of the matter was sublime - effortless even, as though it was something he had practised in the mirror before leaving his quarter of a million pound home in the morning. Tyler continued to listen to him as he delivered his speech, knowing exactly how empty his well-rehearsed statement was. Each word emitted into the air of the empty meeting room landed as translucent, hollow husks. It was in that moment that Tyler felt the mask begin to slip ever so slightly, but he managed to continue to receive the speech in his relaxed manner. He nodded at the appropriate moments and he even managed a smile that might have been deemed as authentic by the casual onlooker. He shook the hand of his boss and left the stuffy office as though they had just attended a casual lunch together. He proceeded to pick up the few belongings that had adorned his desk; a photograph of his father, a recent birthday card signed by his colleagues and a packet of breath mints. He carefully stored them in his satchel and switched his computer off. He watched as the home page closed down and caught his reflection in the black screen. A flash of panic appeared in his eyes and anxiety gripped his features like he was haunted by the face of an innocent man on death row. An overwhelming sensation of terror seemed to paralyse the shape of his mouth in an obtuse tight-lipped expression, as though he was suppressing a primal scream that would rip the office apart like a seismic event intent on obliterating the world. He turned away and began to make his way out of the office. Some of his colleagues said goodbye while others bowed their heads to avoid making eye contact with him. He wondered if they felt relieved that it wasn't them that had been made redundant and they didn't want him to see their guilty expressions as he made his final departure out of the office - the office that had become his second home for the past eight years. He passed through reception and exited by the double doors at the entrance of the building. It felt no different to leaving at the end of a normal working day only to inevitably return the following morning. Yet Tyler would not be returning this time. The speed of his severance had rendered him incapable of fully accepting the news. Looking back on his time working for the company, he had been aware that there may have been one or two warning signs leading up to his departure but he hadn't prepared himself for the worst possible outcome.

On a standard day, Tyler would normally take a fifteen minute walk to the train station before boarding a carriage to continue his journey home. However, on this particular day he proceeded to stroll through the surrounding neighbourhood in a bid to clear his thoughts and to attempt to process the news. The office was located adjacent to a residential area that he had been unfamiliar with for the entire eight years he had been with the company. In fact, in all the time he had worked for Gormans Ltd, he had never thought to explore the area in which he commuted to five days a week. It merely hadn't existed to him. As he followed his feet, he noticed that there was a switch in the sense of his reality upon witnessing the normal homes of the residents nearby. Their houses appeared flawless with their freshly mowed lawns and garden decorations. It was the suburban wet dream and Tyler envisioned the wives of Stepford locked behind the closed doors, baking pies for their adulterous husbands and obnoxious children. He continued to walk, his erratic footsteps matched the beat of his heart until he found himself pausing at one particular building. It was a three storey detached house with a side-built garage attached to the kitchen. A red bricked driveway led up to a gloriously large scarlet front door. The garden borders beckoned and bloomed with luscious wildflowers and foliage that had been trimmed to an inch of perfection. But as his gaze drifted from the fine exterior, his eyes became aware of something through the large window of the dining room. Tyler's feet were immediately rooted to the point directly in front of the house and he was suddenly aware of the palpitations he was experiencing. His breath came and went in short hot heavy blasts and a thin layer of perspiration coated his forehead. The realisation that he had lost his livelihood suddenly hit him in that moment. As he struggled to accept that notion, he thought about the eviction notice he had received a week earlier and the words of his lover claiming that he no longer wanted to be with him any more. The culmination of these little heartbreaks paralysed each and every fibre in his body. His brain became noisy with the swirling thoughts - a thousand voices told him how worthless he was and how it was his fault that he had lost everything.

The mask had fallen away.

He continued to stare through the dining room window of this one particular house that had drawn his attention and he became aware of the silhouette of one of the housewives. Her body slowly rotated from the cable that had been tied around her slender neck and attached to the brass light fixture. Her macabre suspended slow-motion pirouette appeared to deliver a haunting message. He had become a spectator to something he had not prepared for and as Tyler imagined the faces of her husband and children when they returned to find their dearest mother and wife hanging above the dining room table, he considered what this message could be.

If he hadn't decided to walk down this specific street and stop at the house with the scarlet door and the red-brick driveway, then her fatal decision may not have reached him in the way that it was meant to. Tyler had always been receptive to the signs in his life - things that most people may brush off and ignore or things that seemed far too absurd to be considered as important. From the slight change in the weather or a song that played on the radio at a particular moment, he understood it to be a directional nudge in his choices.

Though he was far from being a religious man, he took these signs as a message from the great bold universe to bolster his reasons for making a decision. And it was in that very moment with his eyes bearing witness to the dead housewife that a message was received. The voices that previously had been tormenting him stopped abruptly and a solitary whisper invaded the silence.

Her message was seductive, *this is the action you must take,* it delicately hushed.

Chapter Two

The morning sun kissed the New York skyline as Lana carefully opened the Juliette-style balcony door and let the early breeze whip her freshly showered hair into a frenzy. She blew the steam off her coffee and took a sip. The sound of heavy traffic and irate cab drivers blasting their horns in the streets below served as a welcoming wake-up call. Lana watched as the businessmen strode across the busy crossings with expressions of importance and the single mothers skilfully dodged the almost stationary vehicles with their buggies in one hand and cellphones in the other. Lana had always relished the calm that her apartment provided compared to the chaos that infinitely unfolded below. She found a specific type of contentment in observing the bustling mechanics of city-life as it erupted on the streets below. For this was the city that never sleeps and her apartment provided a security that could not be attained anywhere else. She didn't need the company of a man, or another person for that matter to make her feel secure - she was comfortable with everything she had already acquired. Lana wrapped her silk nightgown closer to her slim figure and stepped back inside the apartment.

She'd awoken with a sense of calm that morning. It was a feeling she could only associate with childhood -waking up on a Saturday morning, free from the confines of school and lessons, a seemingly endless expanse of freedom at her fingertips and a lack of worry of what the future might bring. In those moments, she owned the world and there was no-one or anything that could take that away from her. It was a warming, comfortable sensation that invigorated her senses and allowed her to count her blessings. Now, in her mid twenties, that feeling had become something of a rare experience but it was more welcomed than ever. She finished off the rest of her coffee and rinsed the mug before switching on the morning news. It seemed that on this very day however, murder, war and fear attempted to overshadow her good mood. In a defiant flick of a switch, she turned the television off and picked up her cellphone.

"Hey Phoebe, how's it going?"

"Lana, Jesus - it's like seven in the morning - how d'ya think it's going?" A tired voice groaned down the other end of the line.

"Sorry, I thought you'd be awake by now. Did you get a chance to email over the details about that job?" Lana asked.

"I didn't, I will do it first thing though," Phoebe replied as she stifled a yawn, "how did things go with you-know-who?"

"Never again. I tell you, I'm done with all of that now. The money's good but some of the guys - jeez, I dunno, they're pretty despicable if I'm honest. Gerry, y'know the one who got married two months ago - well, he brought along this device that's meant to emit - wait for it. Electric shocks!" Lana paused as Phoebe struggled to maintain her outburst of laughter.

"Lanny, I'm so glad you've decided to pursue a new career. I mean, I'll miss the stories but you know how I worry about you."

"I know," Lana sighed and approached the kitchen to brew another coffee.

"This other job is easy money, you get to work your own hours and best of all, you don't even have to leave your apartment."

"Yeah. No more seedy motel rooms," Lana muttered.

"No more seedy motel rooms and the icing on the cake, no more jealous wives and girlfriends," Phoebe let out a long meandering yawning sound, "right, I'm up now, let me get a shower and I'll send all the details over to you."

"Thanks Fi, you're the best."

"I know. Speak later yeah?"

"Yeah, later," Lana hung up the phone and scooped up a large heap of freshly ground coffee beans and deposited them in the coffee machine.

*

The journey home had been filled with dark plans.

Bearing witness to the dead housewife had somehow allowed Tyler to accept the finality of his decision. The notion of ending his life was not something unfamiliar to him as he had secretly visited these type of thoughts on numerous occasions throughout the course of his life. They had first presented themselves during his intensive visits to the hospital for tests and operations and eventually chemotherapy. He had spent a lot of time planning everything right down to the very last detail. It wasn't something he had ever been vocal about but he had found comfort in having at least one thing in his life he could control, especially since the cancer had not been one of them. As the years went by, the secret plans changed and evolved in relation to his situations. Ten years ago, when his life had been blessed with the inclusion of close friends and he had managed to maintain a close relationship with his sister, his intentions had involved the heartbreaking process of writing out individual letters. They were all to be written in a similar way, *don't feel guilty, I love you, this is for the best, move on.* These were the main points and in his lowest moments he had actually taken the time to write out the letters with tears in his eyes and a sensation in his stomach as if he had swallowed a black hole. He'd even spent a few extra pounds to ensure that the letters were on the finest paper and handwritten with a calligraphy pen. He would ensure that there were no mistakes, no crossing out of words, no vague statements - the letters had to be precise and to the point but more importantly, he wanted his loved ones to know that he was confident with his decision. He didn't want to be the man that jumped from the bridge who changed his mind a few seconds before impact. Tyler knew that when the day was to come, there would be no turning back and his final wish would be to write a letter to convey that ending his life was right for him. The expensive paper and precise cursive words were to be a last demonstration of respect for those that knew him. These days, however, his plans had changed and the inclusion of these carefully thought out letters had been omitted. The friends that had stuck by him all those years ago were now strangers and his sister who he had so fondly referred to as his sidekick, had gone on to live a life of her own. He tried not to take it too personally - *life happens,* he told himself. If Tyler was looking for a person to blame then it would only be himself. The notions of suicide were not always present however, he'd gotten by quite fine for most of the time. His job had paid the bills and he had maintained a loving relationship with his partner for over five years so the compulsive thoughts were often relegated to the back of his mind. He could allow himself to attempt to feel a momentary sense of contentment, perhaps even happiness. However, it was too late for any of that now, after seeing the housewife dangling lifelessly from the dining room light fixture, he knew the sign was far too clear to be ignored.

Tyler didn't recall leaving that street. He hadn't even thought to contact the police to report what he had witnessed. Instead, he had left her suspended in her final pose - her head hung loosely upon her exposed collar bone, her wilted arms solemnly pointed towards the floor and a slight rotation of her body - a final dance out of this plane of existence. Tyler considered that she wanted to be found that way and who was he to strip her of her final wish? He could only respect her will, though he tried to banish the images of her family returning home to find her suspended above the dining room table. He didn't want to imagine their faces contorted into various shapes of horror, forever reliving that bloodcurdling moment for the rest of their lives. He shuddered at what he had done but his mind had been too preoccupied with the delivery of the message that reporting his discovery had not been a priority in that moment.

Tyler had found that researching suicide methods had become something of a morbid hobby. He had extensively searched online to find out which would be the quickest, most painless way of committing this final act since no one in their right mind wanted to leave this world in a violent and painful manner. Tyler didn't want anything to go awry, he had read various horror stories of people blasting away the majority of their faces only to come around, slightly dazed yet still alive and breathing. He recalled reports of those that had not tied the knot in the noose in the correct manner and had unfortunately proceeded to endure a slow strangulation before the rope eventually gave away due to their frantic body spasms.

If he was going to kill himself, he only wanted to do it once.

The walk from the station to his apartment in the lower east side of the city was nothing more than a blur of passing faces. Faces of desperate people - pain and addiction seemed to glow from beneath the whites of their sunken eyes. Faces of gaunt, tired looking people desperate for a change slipped in and out of flickering neon takeaways and smoky pubs. Tyler had often looked at these people and felt a certain amount of compassion for them but he had never taken the time to talk to them. His compassion was tainted with a certain degree of distrust and a self-preserving sense of survival. The same day he had accepted his fate was the same day he realised he had become one of them. His creased features had become a reflection of theirs and his steps failed to do nothing more than scrape the pavement as a solitary march of an undead creature with no sense of a destination.

Tyler's apartment was located on the top floor of a building that housed an Indian takeaway restaurant and two additional apartments below his. The only access to his floor was via three levels of stairwells which were often inhabited by the occasional shifty-looking character lurking in one of the corners and the lingering aroma of a greasy chicken madras. Tyler had considered himself lucky that he had never encountered any form of discernible trouble despite the number of times he had been the recipient of some version of a defamatory comment or the occasional curse word. As Tyler turned the corner to continue up to his level, he passed a man in a black hooded sweatshirt. The hood had been pulled right over his head but his eyes were clearly distinguishable as they glared from underneath. They were the eyes of someone who hadn't slept in a week and thin red spidery veins sprawled across the white surface. The pupils were no larger than the dots that hovered in the letter 'i' and as Tyler passed him, he grumbled something incoherently.

He spoke again, "some of them know, y'know?" the hooded man groaned, "they know and you'll never be able to see their faces. Not now, not anymore. They know-"

Tyler paid no attention to the comments, it was evident that the man was undoubtedly strung out on something or just plain drunk. He continued up to his apartment and unlocked the front door, as he stepped inside the dark hallway he was greeted with the familiar smell of damp and cologne that immediately clung to the lining of his nostrils.

This is it, he thought, *the next time I'll be leaving this apartment will be in a body bag.* The thought caused him to shudder but he was tired now and the thought of starting his life over again was nothing but unbearable. He flicked the entry light on and realised he was standing on something - it was an envelope. On inspection, the small square envelope contained nothing more than Tyler's full name and address. There was no return address provided on the back-side, only a series of stamps plastered across the front. The flap had been taped down with brown scotch tape that was bubbled and creased as though sealed in a rush. He was baffled as to why the postman would have traipsed all the way up three storeys to slide the envelope under his door when there was a post box on the lower level for all the residential apartments. He put no more thought into it and carefully tore open the envelope. Inside was a single piece of letter paper, the faint outlines of handwriting in black ink could be seen on the reverse. Tyler unfolded the paper and scanned the name at the bottom, *Tara Hamilton.* His heart suddenly began to pound in his chest, *why was his sister writing to him?* They had always been on a similar wavelength and he immediately wondered if she had beat him to it - perhaps she had taken her life and mailed this letter just as he had originally planned all those years ago. The way she had signed the letter seemed so formal and he knew straight away that something wasn't right. He took a deep breath in an attempt to calm his racing heart before he began to read the contents of the note.

Dear Tyler,

I wanted to say that I hope you are well and that life is treating you kindly. I've been thinking about you a lot recently. I moved a couple of years ago to a little town a few miles outside of the Lake District called Edenville. I've managed to rent a little house on a quiet street, it's surrounded by miles and miles of fields and greenery. I understand you must be busy but I was hoping that you would come and visit as soon as possible. I'd be delighted to show you around and catch up with you after all this time. It's been too long. Come and visit.

Yours sincerely,
Tara Hamilton

Beneath her name she had scribbled her new address but she had not provided a contact telephone number. There was something odd about the letter, for a start, it just didn't sound like his sister. The tone was far too jovial and pleasant, they'd grown up together and they had never ceased using the odd nickname or profanity when addressing each other, it had become something of an inside joke between them. Tyler also struggled to imagine Tara ever beginning a letter with the word 'dear', it wasn't part of her vocabulary, especially if she was to ever write a letter. The content was also far too bland for someone who had been a self-acclaimed rebel from a young age. Her spelling was usually atrocious and she had often commented that it didn't matter how something was spelt, as long as it was understood. Yet the letter contained not a single typo or grammatical error. He read the letter a few more times to try and decipher some other hidden meaning but came back with no further clue. There was very little more he could squeeze from the small amount of hand-written words. Tyler walked through into his tiny kitchen, the overhead fluorescent light hummed to life after a few electrical clicks and he took a seat on a stool by the counter. The letter had become slightly creased and dampened from his firm grip and perspiring palms.

"There has to be more to this," he said aloud to himself, realising that the day seemed to delivering him conflicting cryptic messages.

It had to be far too much of a coincidence that he would receive a letter from his estranged sister whom he had not seen in over eight years on the very day that he was planning to end his life. The letter itself had been too unusual for him to ignore, *maybe she was in trouble? Perhaps this was some sort of hidden plea for help?* He wished he could pick up his phone and call her to retrieve more answers but he had lost her number many years ago and had never thought to establish contact again. A pang of guilt fell upon him, *I should've stayed in touch,* he realised. He began to pace the small room, rubbing his furrowed brow anxiously, *I've not got nothing more to lose,* he thought, *I've already lost everything else, there's no harm in taking one last trip and then I can come back and finish the deed.* He nodded in agreement with himself, *yes - that's what I'll do, I'll visit Tara, I'll find out the real reason for this letter, I'll say goodbye in person and then... And then... I can finally call it quits.*

Chapter Three

Lana refreshed the computer screen only to receive an email with a discount coupon for a new organic food store that had just opened up a few blocks away. She had still not received the promised message from Phoebe causing her to sigh deeply as she closed the laptop. The sun had now fully risen and the light in the apartment felt otherworldly. She glanced around the room, her possessions were minimal and sparse. Since the age of eighteen, Lana had only acquired what she needed and found that living hand-to-mouth had its own perks. For starters, she was able to save up and afford the spacious apartment she resided in or she could choose to eat at a nice restaurant if that was something she so wished to do one particular evening. She relished in the knowledge that she was financially secure by working the sort of jobs that she did, although that sort of security wasn't always favourable to some girls in the business. She had considered herself to be lucky and it didn't do any harm that she had the bone structure of a super-model and the intelligence of a genetic research technician. Lana was lucky and she had never once taken her blessings for granted.

In an attempt to keep busy, she swiftly picked up her keys and purse from the kitchen counter and made her way out of the apartment.

"Good morning Mrs Fuller, how's Chi Chi today?" Lana waved at an elderly lady carrying a rolled up newspaper in one arm and a tiny Chihuahua in the other as she was just about to step into her apartment a little farther down the hallway.

"Oh good mornin' Lana dear, he's been a little restless lately but I think those meds are starting to work," she called across in a volume that was a little louder than necessary.

"I'm happy to hear that, you take care Mrs Fuller!" Lana shouted back before continuing down the hallway.

She arrived at the elevator and pressed the button with the icon of a downward arrow. As she entered the confined carriage, she had a sudden feeling that she had forgotten something. Patting down her side pockets, she could feel that her keys, phone and purse were all present and correct but she could not shake the distinct feeling that something was out of place. She arrived in the lobby and greeted Bobby at reception, he tipped his cap as she walked past and she returned the gesture with a beaming smile and a warm morning salutation. Bobby rarely spoke and his silent gestures had become something of legend within the apartment complex. When he did speak, his words were drenched in a cool, southern drawl that might have sounded out of place in the middle of the city yet it was perfectly paired with the distinct out-of-town feeling of the interior design of the building.

Lana stepped out into the busy street, the blaring honking and heavy pollutants were more intense on ground level but she breathed it all in. The city had been her home for all her life even though she had been passed from family to family as a toddler and right through her troublesome teenage years. New York became the maternal figure she had so desperately craved. She joined the fast pace march of pedestrians and efficiently turned in to Raj's Seven-Eleven convenience store. The aisles were stocked with numerous colourful packets and packages and Lana made her way to the large refrigerators at the rear of the shop. She grabbed a carton of rice milk and as she turned to make her way to the check-out she caught sight of her reflection in the stainless steel exterior of the refrigerator. It was a blurry configuration of her facial features though she instantly recognised her luminous blue eyes and the way her hair curled around her earlobes when she hadn't taken the time to carefully blow-dry it a particular way. Although it wasn't her reflection that caused a sharp intake of breath. It was the reflection of the person stood a few steps behind her that caused a chill to pass through her body. She clutched the milk in one hand and found herself squeezing tighter and tighter as she tried to make sense of what she could only perceive as the face of death incarnate lurking directly behind her. Deep dark sockets bore through her, the face - gaunt and tight with a hint of yellow seemed to be trying to extract something from her. *My soul,* she thought. Lana considered herself to be a sensible girl and hadn't bothered her mind with any beliefs of the supernatural world yet in that moment, something disturbed her to the core. She felt a certainty that the Grim Reaper had approached her in Raj's Seven-Eleven to rip out her soul with his well-concealed scythe. Lana took a deep breath as she began to turn to face her opponent. Terror engulfed her nerves as she looked deep into the dark recesses of his eyes. They appeared to be endlessly deep and she was scared that if she looked too far into them that she might encounter a whole new level of horror within them. As she pulled her gaze back, it became apparent that her initial assumption that the figure behind her was the Grim Reaper may have been slightly off kilter. The man had a hood pulled up over his head, strands of greasy grey-black hair hung out from underneath in matted clumps. His face was square and hollow and he appeared to be perspiring heavily, that or there had been a sudden downpour outside. His hands were tucked in the front two pockets of his jacket as he continued to glare at her. Lana quickly quashed the worst part of her fear and began to move past him. As Lana took a step in his direction, his mouth puckered up and he began to make a slurping sound as though he was inhaling through an invisible straw. She squeezed her face up in disgust at his actions and began to walk away but he continued to make the strange sucking sound. The volume of the grotesque noise grew louder as she moved farther away from him. Arriving at the checkout, she turned to see if he had followed her but he had remained in the exact same position looking straight in her direction with his piercing coal-like eyes. His mouth was still puckered and he continued to make the grotesque sound. Lana placed a five dollar bill down on the counter and informed the clerk to keep the change. She almost mentioned her bizarre experience with the stranger at the back of the store to the store assistant but realised there was very little use in reporting something that was just plain strange but evidently harmless. She had encountered even crazier people in the past, it was just part and parcel of living in a big city and she was at least grateful that this one hadn't tried to grab her or do anything worse. Yet she could not shake the image of his bottomless eyes. They seemed to follow her all the way back to her apartment.

*

Tyler hadn't made much progress in packing for his trip, he'd opened up a suitcase and had managed to load it with a few pairs of socks, underwear, a travel toothbrush and a hairbrush that had seen better days. He looked down at the lonesome items as he continued to dissect the contents of the letter. There was an abstract part of him that had been grateful for the distraction. After witnessing the lifeless body of the housewife, his brain had been plagued with a debilitating darkness and although he still wanted to depart from his life, the contact from his sister had ignited a small spark of life inside of him. The idea of a final adventure seemed to soften the edges of his harsh plans. It seemed to offer a temporary relief that he would not have been able to have summoned himself. There was still the distinct feeling that something was a little unusual about the letter and he had spent the better part of the last forty five minutes trying to locate a hidden clue or code-word within the short passage. He recalled exchanging numerous greeting cards and letters with his sister in the past but he still could not be sure whether the handwriting matched hers or not. He scanned the contents of the letter one last time before carefully folding it along the creases and sliding it behind the hairbrush. *What's going on with her? Why the mysterious letter?* He felt a moment of relief in accepting that these questions overshadowed the fatal thoughts from early on.

Chapter Four

Lana had returned to the apartment and locked the door behind her. She hadn't acknowledged Bobby as she walked through the lobby, nor did she acknowledge the new family that had been wheeling large crates and packages into a newly empty apartment. Her mind was preoccupied with the encounter in the convenience store. It wasn't unusual to come across people who were clearly going through some form of personal struggle when she was out in the city and she was fairly accustomed to witnessing them acting out in particular ways. Sometimes the cops would turn up, but most of the time they wouldn't. Big cities had a habit of attracting all walks of life. There are those that gravitate to a horizon filled with large skyscrapers and industrial history, clinging to a promise of change, while others merely end up there - discarded and desolate like garbage bags lining the side-streets. Either way, once you enter a place like New York, it becomes very difficult to leave. Lana had been born with the city branded on her heart yet she had never encountered anyone with such a foreboding presence like the man in the convenience store. It had been as though he was attempting to reach deep inside of her, intent on feasting on a part of her that for so long, had been chained to a wall in a catacomb of personal tragedies. Lana knew that revisiting these parts of her was not a good idea, there had been a very good reason why she had buried them deep down and the last thing she wanted to do was to begin digging fresh holes for them after all this time. She tried to push the situation to the back of her mind, so instead of placing the milk in the fridge, she took a seat at

the small glass dining table and flicked open her laptop. She logged in to her
email account to find a message from Phoebe.

Hey! Sorry I know I said I was going to send this
through much sooner but Derek got a little handsy
this morning and I lost track of time. Blame Derek!
The link for the job and the initial set up process
is below, use the password SWORDCOINTHREE.
    I've known a few girls who have made some good
money from this and you won't even have to leave your
place. I've attached a pdf of the scripting they use
so it might be worth reading through it all that
before you set up your profile and account. Let me
know if you wanna grab a coffee in the week, I'm in
desperate need of a break. Speak later!!! xo

Lana clicked on the pdf link and downloaded the file to her computer.
Once it had completed, she clicked it open and the first page sprung to life.
'Clara's Online Psychic Emporium: Renowned Intuitive and Fortune Guiders'.
Lana scoured the pages further more, there was a contractual agreement page
which stipulated that anyone revealing any trade secrets would be severely
reprimanded. Lana rolled her eyes as she read more about the agreements and
wondered who would buy into all of this psychic business. It was not
something she had much firsthand experience with and that tended to mean
that she was highly skeptical of it. She had trusted Phoebe's word and had
accepted that the time was right to get out of escorting. Phoebe had known a
number of girls who had matched the money they made escorting by working

for Clara's Emporium. That was the main trouble with being an escort - the money was never steady. Sometimes it would come in like an un-forecast down-fall, other times, Lana was forced to miss a few meals and put off payments for a few bills but she maintained a certain amount of comfort and still managed to maintain the security of a healthy life savings account.

Beneath all the rules and regulations were a few more pages that outlined the scripting procedure and how to persuade potential clients to agree to private readings. The concept of the site seemed relatively simple - Clara's Emporium home page was set up allowing access to a series of different chat rooms, each one designated to a particular intuitive ability. *Clairvoyance - a psychic seeing. Clairsentience - a psychic feeling. Clairaudience - psychic readings made through sound and Claircognizance - an all over psychic knowing.* There were further add-ons such as Tarot readings and palm readings which could be organised via webcam once payment had been received. The idea was to fish a client out from one of the main rooms and have them receive a reading in the form of private messaging with one of Clara's 'highly qualified trained psychic assistants.' Lana had read through a guide on cold reading techniques and realised that she was almost at inauguration level of these 'highly trained psychic assistants.' She was quietly amazed at how much information could be obtained simply by asking a few open-ended questions. The guide explained that the skill was much easier to do in person that it was through a chat room but with practice and confidence it would become second nature. It appeared that *confidence* seemed to be the operative word for Clara's Emporium. She had read that singular word at least half a dozen times and she hadn't even completed reading the guide. Lana shook her head at the thought of so many gullible people who would willingly part with their money in order to hear some made-up spiel from a complete stranger who may not even be qualified enough to look after themselves. The overall concept seemed scandalous and completely immoral but Lana justified it by telling herself, *if people are stupid enough to believe it, then so fool them.*

*

Euston station heaved with activity. People arrived and people departed with suitcases of varying sizes trailing behind them. Business men strode confidently with looks of determination whilst clutching polystyrene coffee cups as though their lives were dependent on a consistent caffeine fix. Tyler stood motionless in front of the departure board, awaiting for an announcement on which platform to board. His eyes glazed over as the seemingly endless lists of destinations and times scrolled and refreshed above him. He had decided against bringing a suitcase and instead had packed a small backpack, he realised that the visit may be a limited one. *What would she say when he turned up unannounced on her doorstep? She might have a family and a fulfilling career now and be too busy to accommodate a visit from her absent brother.* A number of doubts had followed Tyler from his home to the station and he had considered turning back on more than one occasion. He had pulled out the now crumpled letter several times to remind him why he was embarking on the visit and told himself that this was one of two options and the other option had a slightly more fatal outcome.

As he watched the LCD screen update and scroll through the various destinations, Tyler thought back to when he had last seen his sister. It had been Christmas day, back in 2007. A mutual friend of theirs had invited them over for dinner and it had resulted in an excessive binge of burnt turkey and mulled wines. Tyler recalled turning up with a loosely wrapped gift for Tara - a bottle of brandy that he had bought at the last minute. He had also taken the time to buy a Christmas pudding as his contribution to Jake's dinner. There were a few other friends of Jakes that had been invited and by the time that Tyler arrived, they had already settled into their various states of inebriation. The small terraced house had been dressed from top to bottom in tinsel which glistened in an array of different colours, while crude-looking plastic Santa Clauses and reindeers had been stuffed into each and every corner in an attempt to instil some festive cheer. The hallway and kitchen had been brought to life with strings of multi-coloured fairy lights and classic Christmas tunes were being blasted out via the television in the living room which had been propped up on a rickety old upright piano. Tyler had been reminded of his student days and his attendance at numerous raucous freshman parties that either ended with several people being violently sick in the bathroom or someone being rushed to A and E as they had overdosed on whatever drug had been making the rounds that night.

Tara was sat in the kitchen, a large glass of rosé in one hand and a cigarette in the other. She quickly stubbed it out as she noticed Tyler entering the room.

"Tye!" she screamed as she leapt from her seat and ran over to him, she wrapped her arms around him and spilled half of the contents of her glass on the floor in the process. "Never mind that," she said, "how are you bro-ster? I was just talking about you!"

Tara stepped back and looked at him, "you look good, this porn-star moustache suits you little brother," she playfully grabbed at his upper lip.

"I hope you were saying good things about me," Tyler replied, he pulled back as Tara continued to tug at his newly grown facial hair.

"Only ever good things," she smiled, "you know that."

Tyler shifted his attention to a tall long haired man with his hand halfway up the back end of a large pink turkey, "hi Jake, I brought pudding."

"Thanks Tye, although I'm not too sure people are going to last until dessert," Jake smiled and blew away a stray hair that had fallen in front of his face.

"Yeah right," Tyler laughed despite not being sure what he was actually agreeing with, he could feel heat rising to his face and was worried that Jake would notice his blatant attraction so he quickly turned back to Tara. "You good sis?"

Tara moved to the kitchen counter and propped herself against it, "you know how it is," she replied as she began to pour herself another drink.

Tyler nodded in agreement.

The two siblings had been through a fair amount of challenges in their younger years but this had caused their bond had become as strong as reinforced steel. It had been those hardships that had brought them closer together.

"Wanna drink?" she asked.

"Fuck yes," Tyler replied emphatically, he opened his mouth and rolled his eyes back to symbolise being parched.

"All passengers for Oxenholme thirteen fifteen, please make your way to platform six, that's all passengers departing to Oxenholme, thirteen fifteen, please make your way to platform six."

The announcement brought Tyler back from his memory. He could still smell the combined aroma of cinnamon-scented candles, wine and roast potatoes from that day. Though the majority of that afternoon remained as a vivid recollection, the late afternoon and evening had descended into a blurry mess.

He inhaled forcefully, as though attempting to rinse the memory out of his body with a mouthful of cleansing air and began to make his way to platform six. A tendril of anxiety was beginning to uncoil in his body and his heart rate increased slightly.

"Just keep going," he whispered to himself.

Chapter Five

It had just past noon when Lana awoke from a short nap, the whirlwind of different dreams had rendered her exhausted. The strange encounter in the convenience store had triggered a surreal expedition through landscapes of men making obscene noises at her as she traversed a hot sandy desert. A purple sky raged with thunder storms and her bare feet were slowly being eaten away by the blistering hot sand. She looked down to see her ankles had been stripped down to nothing more than chalky white bone and weeping red flesh. Despite her semi-awareness that is was merely only a dream, the pain seared through her body unlike any sort of pain she had experienced before. It seemed to burn and rage through every cell of her being. As she continued to walk through the desolate land, her feet began to fall apart in thick bloody clumps and she struggled to maintain her balance upon the stumps that was left remaining of her legs. A crowd of men in hoods and puckered up faces appeared in the clouds and taunted her as she fell into a tired heap in the sand, cradling the sore remnants of her limbs. Though her screams seemed to tear her chest apart, not a sound could be heard across this obsolete dream-world. Lana knew that she was alone in the suffering and in that moment, a particular knowledge that this was always meant to be her fate descended upon her but she wouldn't allow the tears to come.

Lana quickly sat up on the sofa, her eyes were wet and her heart thudded in her chest. She flicked her wrist over and looked at her watch, amazed to discover that she had only been asleep for an hour. Thinking back to the horrifying desert pilgrimage, she realised she had felt quite disengaged from the world for at least a few days. She allowed the dreams to sink to the bottom of her stomach, yet they felt heavy and dense inside of her. Lana knew that the memories of them would dissolve in time yet she shuddered at the thought of holding on to them, cursed to eternally relive those horrifying images.

In an attempt to distract herself, she grabbed her laptop and logged into Clara's Emporium and continued to complete her profile. The process was relatively straight forward, she had settled for a name that sounded both mysterious and exotic - *Orla*. There was the option to upload a photograph but she had decided against it for now - she wasn't sure she wanted to attach an image of herself to something she believed to be a public display of mockery. She spent a little more time looking into the chatrooms to get a sense of what to expect. They didn't appear as active as she had first thought but she contemplated that it may have been due to the fact that it was the early afternoon. Twenty five so-called psychics had been logged in and she counted only eight guests. Some of them sent desperate messages wishing to contact loved ones that had passed on or sought advice on their failing lives. As Lana navigated through the chatrooms, she felt nothing but despair reading the messages. The alleged psychics used various fishing tactics to reach out to the guests, offering scripted promises that Lana had recognised from the 'user-manual' she had read earlier. Of course these promises were only to be dispensed after the production of a MasterCard number. One user sent her a direct message provoking Lana to quickly log off and she decided to let the idea of ripping people off sit with her for a while. At least when she was escorting, her customers were getting something relatively genuine in return. As she debated how to spend the rest of the day, she heard a soft knocking come from the front door - she hadn't been expecting any visitors. Still groggy from the nap, she wrapped a dressing gown around her and shuffled to the door. The soft rapping was constant, as though a small bird was attempting to peck a hole right through the reinforced wood. She used the spy-hole to see who it was that so desperately wanted her attention. The face of a young man looked straight back at her, his eyes were unlike anything she had ever seen before. At first glance, they appeared to be the most brilliant blue sapphire gemstones with a wavering light caught inside them, yet they also glowed with a strange fluorescent green hue. Lana couldn't be sure if it was a trick of the light or whether she was still half asleep but the startling look of his eyes made her body run cold.

"Can I help you?" she called through the door.

"Hello?" he stopped the incessant knocking. His voice was deep and didn't seem to match the young man she saw before her.

"Yeah hi, is there something I can do for you?" Lana asked, she had carefully placed the chain on the door in an attempt to reduce the anxious feeling that was creeping upon her.

"I'm here now, let me in," he said.

"I think you have the wrong apartment."

"No, this is the right apartment," the man stared straight at her through the spy hole, Lana knew that he couldn't see her but his glare seemed to penetrate through the combination of wood and glass and bury itself deep inside of her.

"I don't know who you are." she called out, 'you have the wrong apartment.'

"No," he slammed both of his fists against the door and Lana stumbled back slightly from the shock.

"H-hey, listen this isn't the right apartment. You're probably on the wrong floor," Lana tried to control the shakiness in her voice but the shock of his reaction had rattled her.

The man didn't reply, he continued to stare straight at the door, his gaze had shifted downwards and Lana began to panic, *he's looking at the door handle,* she thought.

"Did you hear me? You have the wrong place," she called out.

He made no response.

She began to make a mental note of his appearance, short brown hair, goatee, pierced ear, neck tattoo - the tail end of a snake perhaps.

It was at that moment that Lana saw the door handle begin to turn.

"Hey!" she raised her volume, "I said, this is the wrong apartment!" Her body began to shake with fear. "Justin! Can you come on over here, there's a guy trying to get into the apartment!" Lana knew it was a cheap shot but it was a trick some of the other escorts had used in the past. They would pretend to have a boyfriend waiting for them in case a punter got a little out-of-hand. The trick appeared to work, the handle flicked back up into its resting position and Lana felt her breath return. She approached the spy hole once again and saw nothing but the empty hallway. Resting against the door, she waited for her heart to slow down. She had never been aware of any situations like this occurring in the complex. Bobby, despite his silent demeanour was extremely vigilant and would never allow anyone in the building unless they were a resident or a guest that appeared to be of sane mind. The young man that had been at her door was most certainly neither of those. She checked through the spy hole once more to ensure that he hadn't returned and she made a snap decision to get out of the apartment.

*

Tyler had taken a seat in the unreserved section away from any other passengers. He wanted to be alone and watch the rolling landscape whilst he attempted to collect his thoughts. He tucked his backpack under his seat and watched the train as it pulled away from the station and began to accelerate. There was something cathartic about watching the grey, slab-like city transform into endless fields of countryside. Living in the city for so long had made Tyler forget what the rest of the country looked like. The occasional farm or cottage house reminded him that there was more to life outside of the industrial sphere that he had gotten far too accustomed to.

Tyler dozed off briefly and awoke abruptly to find that the carriage was no longer empty. A stocky man had taken a seat opposite him and appeared to be grinning at the fact that Tyler had woken with such a start. He quickly sat up straight and forced his concentration out of the window.

"Where you headin'?"

Tyler heard the man but wasn't sure he was speaking to him so he pretended he didn't hear and continued to watch the greenery flash past the window.

"Sorry, I know it's a little weird, a stranger asking where you're heading to. You start to think, why are they asking me this? Are they out to get me? I was just trying to make some conversation."

Tyler realised that it was himself that was being addressed, he craned his neck slightly and widened his eyes, "I'm sorry, I thought you might have been on your phone," Tyler said, "I wasn't being rude," he forced a short fake laugh to reinforce his statement.

"No harm done," the man replied.

Tyler made eye contact and realised why he had tried not to acknowledge the man sat opposite him. There was aura of kindness that surrounded him, it reminded him of Ben and anything that sparked those sort of memories provoked stabbing pains in his chest and stomach - he was still adjusting to single life.

"Edenville," Tyler said, "that's where I'm going. What about you?"

"Nowhere as glamorous as somewhere called Edenville, I've never heard of it. It sounds kinda biblical," he chuckled to himself, "I'm Geoff by the way."

"Tyler - or Tye, whichever you prefer," Tyler responded.

"Tye's cool, I'll stick with that. So what's important in Edenville?"

"I'm visiting family. Been a while," Tyler answered, averting Geoff's gaze.

"Cool," he flashed a half smile and Tyler felt the blood in his body pump just a little bit faster and a littler bit warmer.

"Are you?"

"Am I?"

"Sorry," Tyler felt himself growing bashful, "are you visiting family?"

"An old friend, in Manchester. I've not seen him in a couple of years, I've been travelling with work and keeping busy." Geoff replied.

"I see."

Despite the fact that Geoff was wearing an oversized baseball cap, Tyler could make out his chiselled jawline, a weeks worth of stubble and dark eyes that contained a certain amount of history. This made him a little nervous.

"You want the rest of my coffee? I've had about two sips," Geoff held out a white polystyrene cup and Tyler politely refused.

"Very wise, I always seem to get the train station coffee before I remember how bad it is. I guess it's one of the downsides of travelling." Geoff stated as he placed the cup firmly in the cup holder.

"Bad beverages," Tyler enthused and instantly wondered why he felt that comment was necessary, he saw Geoff smile slightly and breathed a sigh of relief.

"So, are you staying in Edenville for the weekend?"

"I'm not sure yet. My sister doesn't know I'm coming so it could be a short stay."

"A surprise visit. They tend to be the best kind of visits," Geoff said, "I like surprises, you know, even if it's something you don't like, I think the act of being surprised is pretty special."

"Every day is a surprise," Tyler added, realising he had used a similar motto when he had been undergoing chemotherapy. Although those years seemed like a completely different time, as though he had lived an entirely different life, but every now and again he would remember that voice that would come to him, willing him to be stronger and to tackle a new day. That in itself had been a surprise.

"Yeah, I like that. Every day certainly is a surprise," Geoff nodded as he pondered the statement, "y'know Tye, I think you might have been a philosopher in a former life."

"I doubt that very much," he laughed.

"You shouldn't doubt yourself," Geoff replied, his tone had taken a slightly more serious tone, morose even, as though he was speaking to a hidden part of himself.

"You're right," Tyler said, "self doubt serves no purpose, it just ends up holding you back."

Geoff flashed him that charming half smile once more and Tyler chuckled to himself, "I think you might be right, maybe I was a bit of a philosopher in a past life."

Chapter Six

Lana sipped a dry martini as she observed her environment. She had been to Miami's several times and found the decorum to have the right balance - not too many hipster fakers but just enough to keep it interesting. It was a little past three, and although she considered that the casual onlooker may look down upon a girl in her late twenties drinking in the afternoon, in a place like Miami's, no one cared. There were enough functioning drunks in the bar to cast a neutral vibe that didn't make anyone feel guilty about partaking in a cocktail or two before the sun had begun to set. After a few drinks, it didn't seem to matter anyway. Lana was attempting to flush the events of the day away but her martini hadn't served to dispel the memories. She kept replaying the incident in the convenience store and the altercation at her apartment in her head. As Lana had left the apartment complex, she had asked Bobby about the man that had come to her door, but he didn't recall seeing such a person. He promised to check out the security tapes to see if he could find out who he was and how he got to her floor, although Lana had asked him not to go to such trouble. Her bizarre dream seemed to act as the strange adhesive that held the events of the day together. It was as though it had somehow changed a part of her. She knew the feeling would soon dissipate and had hoped the martini would have sped up the process but it only seemed to shake up the events in her mind as she was sifting sand on the hunt for precious minerals. *What was the meaning behind of all this?* She pondered.

"Can I get you another?" the bartender asked.

"Sure." Lana replied and finished off the rest of her glass.

Miami's was an eighties neon-fusion throwback bar, complete with plastic palm trees and fluorescent cable lights that flickered and flashed in an offbeat manner. The music was predominantly eighties pop and the bar hosted Karaoke every Friday and Saturday night. Although Lana had yet to bear witness to those delights. Instead, she enjoyed the pastiche nature and the affordable-but-not-cheap drinks. The bartender passed her another martini and she took a sip, relishing the chill as it passed her lips. A hand tapped her on the shoulder and she turned around to greet Phoebe, she immediately stood to embrace her.

"That's some weird shit right there, Lanny. This is why I hate the fact that you live all by yourself, the crazies seem to sniff out the single ladies like wild dogs in heat," Phoebe finished the last of her beer and placed the bottle down on a coaster shaped like a mini vinyl record.

They had moved to a table in the corner of the bar and Lana had spent the previous twenty minutes filling Phoebe in on her eventful day.

"It's just so strange, I've lived in New York my entire life and yes, I've encountered one or two characters but I don't normally feel as though I am being-" Lana took a deep breath, "I dunno-targeted, I guess," she said. "I know it sounds completely paranoid but it feels like someone is out for me. Those two weird guys-"

"I don't think you're being targeted, it's just an unlucky coincidence, nothing more will happen," Phoebe paused, "but, if anything does, don't even hesitate to call the cops. Y'know that's what they're there for. Right?"

Lana looked glumly down at her now-empty martini glass.

"Right?" Phoebe repeated, emphasising the fact that she was asking a question and not making a statement.

Lana raised her head and managed a weak smile, "right," she repeated.

"Did you check out that job?" Phoebe asked, skilfully changing the topic to lighten the mood.

"Yeah-" Lana started but couldn't find the words to express her thoughts on the matter.

"Well?" Phoebe probed, "easy cash maker, am I right?"

Lana glanced down at her glass again.

"Are you seriously gonna make me repeat every single question tonight? That shit gets old real fast."

"Sorry," Lana said as she quickly shook her hair loose, "you're right, I need to snap out of it, it's just everything that's happened has freaked me out. So yeah, the job-" she paused once more. "I'm just not sure I can rip people off like that, it seems kinda dishonest."

"Look Lanny, everyone knows that psychics are a bunch of fake asses but it doesn't stop them from seeking them out. It clearly states on the website that it's for entertainment purposes only. It's their fault if they don't get what that means," Phoebe turned to wave at the bartender to bring her over another drink.   Lana had known Phoebe for just over ten years, they had met at high school and had soon hit it off as close friends. They shared all aspects of their lives with each other and despite Lana's resilient exterior, it was Phoebe that had the balls and a rational perspective of the world. She was the kind of girl that would be perfectly happy leaving the apartment in her pyjamas and her hair tied up in a loose bun intent on going about her day but her job required her to look semi professional. Although she would still display her rebellious side with her various nose piercings and arm tattoos on full display at any given opportunity.

"I just feel like it's taking advantage of people at a vulnerable time. It makes me a little uncomfortable," Lana explained.

"I get it. I really do, and if you don't wanna do it then by all means, don't do it, no harm done. I just wanna make sure you're safe, y'know? Escorting doesn't lead to promotions and you can't do it forever. Lana you're a smart girl, remember how you'd ace all the exams in school? I just know that you're capable of more-"

The bartender interrupted Phoebe as he placed a fresh beer down in front of her, "thanks," she said and turned back to Lana, "I don't wanna see you get yourself in any trouble. I mean that guy that showed up at your apartment, he might know what you do, it might be linked-" Phoebe paused. "I'm not trying to scare you Lanny, I just want you to be safe." She reached over and placed her hand on top of Lana's. "You hear those stories every now and again-"

"I know. Thank you." Lana smiled, "I'm always very safe, I never use my own place, no one knows my real name or where I live. I take all the necessary precautions."

"I know you do Lanny, but you can take all the precautions in the world and still something bad can happen."

Lana didn't respond.

"Just think about it okay. It wasn't easy getting you that job, they don't just let anyone sign up you know." Phoebe took a swig and flashed her a devilish grin, "I say we make this an all-nighter, wha'd'ya say?"

*

The train pulled away from Oxenholme train station and Tyler offered a quick wave to Geoff who had moved over to the window seat to bid him farewell. They had spent the remainder of the journey talking about many different topics, though their personal lives had been left clearly off the table. It was almost as though they were both protecting something that they were not sure they were willing to share just yet. Before Tyler had gotten off at his station, Geoff had insisted that he took his number and get in touch after his visit. Tyler had been a little reluctant but realised there was no harm in doing so and exchanged his number also. He adjusted his backpack and watched as the train disappeared out of view, he felt somewhat vulnerable by himself in an unknown place. The conversations with Geoff had served as a pleasant distraction to the innumerable thoughts he probably would have endured on the journey. He was at least thankful for that and made his way out of the station.

"Where you headin'?"

Tyler had gotten into the first taxi cab that had become available, it had pulled up just in time as the clouds had turned dark and rain had begun to fall.

"Edenville central, Cemetery Road," Tyler said as he got into the back and clicked the seatbelt into position.

"Edenville?" The driver questioned.

"Yeah you know it?" Tyler asked.

"Sure, yeah-"

Tyler wasn't sure whether the driver had questioned him because he hadn't heard him correctly or whether it was rare that he took trips out to that region.

"What's it like?" Tyler questioned, "Edenville?"

"You not been there before eh?" The driver looked at him through the rearview mirror and squinted his eyes.

Tyler shook his head.

"Ah," the driver commented, 'it's nice. Got that- what d'ya call it - that small town charm."

"Sounds nice."

"Yeah, don't tend to get too many people visiting there, a lot of the townsfolk like to keep to themselves, you know how it is," he croaked. He had the voice of a man who had spent a lifetime chain-smoking and drinking high percentage liquors.

Tyler nodded again, he was beginning to sense that the driver was holding something back from him. He quickly got out his phone and ran a search on the town. He found a few pieces about it including some photographs of the town itself. The town had a standard settlement history and it looked like any other small picturesque town in the Cumbria region. He couldn't find any reports of anything that might have been deemed as unusual or untoward. The driver switched the radio on to break the silence that had descended upon the interior of the taxi. In the very same moment that a weather update was being announced, the skies opened up completely and heavy rain began to pound the roof and windows of the cab. A flash of lightning illuminated the sky and thunder roared overhead causing the radio to cut out into static. Another flash of lightning coursed over the blackened horizon. Tyler could make out the jagged elongated rods as they joined the heavens and earth together in an ultimate spark of fury. As quickly as it had flashed in the sky, it was gone again. A few moments passed and the thunder boomed once more.

"Quite a storm. They didn't forecast anything like this this morning!" The driver shouted over the noise of the static on the radio and the thunderous outbursts above.

Tyler didn't respond, instead he watched the long streaks of rain run down the glass and tried to focus his attention on the window screen wipers as they rhythmically waved left to right. He didn't want to acknowledge the knot that was growing tighter and tighter in his stomach and the heavy sensation in his chest. He closed his eyes to try and calm himself and thought of Tara.

"Stay down." She commanded in a hushed whisper.

"Why?" Tyler replied.

"We're just playing a game, like hide and seek but we have to be more serious this time."

"I don't like this," he said, hot tears were beginning to well up behind his eyes and he pushed himself further against the wall.

Tara propped a chair up against the bedroom door, making sure the handle couldn't move before she came back over to Tyler. She crouched down next to him and wrapped one arm around his shoulder. "It's gonna be alright little brother, don't worry," she pulled him in closer.

"What's going on downstairs?" Tyler asked, he could feel the floorboards reverberating beneath him with the bass-line of the music below.

"Mum's just got some of her friends over again. Nothing to worry about. We're just gonna stay up here and play hide and seek. It'll be more fun this way." Tara offered him a reassuring smile.

"Why do we have to turn the lights off though?"

"To make it more fun!" Tara said, but even at six years old, Tyler could tell when his sister was lying to him.

"She's drunk again isn't she?" he said, he could feel the tears begin to choke him and his voice shook as he spoke the words.

"You know that no matter what happens Tye, you'll always have me, okay?"

Tyler felt the tears begin to roll down his cheeks.

"You're never gonna be alone Tye, you know that, right?" she whispered as she used her pinkie finger to wipe away his tears.

He nodded slowly and tucked his head under her chin, he could feel her long feathery hair tickle his face and she pulled him in closer.

"We're a team, you and I. Us against the world," she whispered as she began to slowly rock him.

A loud smash erupted downstairs in the living room and the sound of heavy footsteps could be heard clumsily stamping up the stairs. The music below seemed to increase in volume as the footsteps got closer. They stopped directly outside the room and someone began to smash at the door. Tara slowly rose to a standing position as they witnessed it begin to come away from the frame with each loud bang. The chair she had propped up was beginning to lose its position and slide away from the door. Tara took a step forward before turning back to Tyler and whispered, "stay right there and remember, I'm not going to let anyone hurt you, Tye. It's you and me against the world remember," she gave him another smile but Tyler could see the fear in her eyes. It was something he didn't see in her too often, she turned away from him as the door crashed open.

"Here we go."

The voice was harsh and stripped the image of the bedroom away.

"Cemetery Road, Edenville."

Tyler snapped his eyes open and it took a moment for him to acknowledge the interior of the taxi once more.

The driver had turned slightly in his seat and was looking directly at him.

"Right, yeah thanks, how much?" Tyler asked, his eyes were still adjusting to the light. The storm had broken and the skies had returned to a pale blue, a few wispy clouds could be seen overhead but the sun had appeared to have melted the rest away.

"Sixty five, ninety five," the driver said tapping the meter in front of him.

Tyler pulled his wallet out of his backpack and handed him the money, "how long was I asleep for?"

"Maybe 'bout an hour or so."

"Okay," Tyler replied as he signalled for the driver to keep the change. He picked up his back pack and opened the door.

"Enjoy your visit!" The driver croaked as Tyler stepped out on to the pavement.

Chapter Seven

It was two in the morning when Lana first glanced at her watch. After several more drinks in Miami's, the two girls had made their way to a local Chinese takeaway to eat and then moved on to the next bar. They were practically wasted by the time they reached The Eye Ball, a bar that Phoebe swore made the most intricate and unusual cocktails. She had used her relentless charm on the door-man as they had staggered and swayed their way through the entrance. Once inside, they proceeded to make friends with some of the locals and use the dance floor to show off what they believed to be carefully refined moves. For Lana, this was only fuelled and made easier with each drink she downed. By midnight, she had been successful in achieving her goal of forgetting the creepy succession of events throughout the course of the day. The dream and the strange encounters seemed like scenes she had observed from someone else's life. Phoebe, though taken, had flirted shamelessly with a number of different people, both male and female. This was the old version of Phoebe that Lana had partied with in college, the reckless and adored girl who showed not a single worry in the world. She had envied her ability to not allow anything in and affect her. It was one of the things that had first drawn Lana to her.

"Hey Fi, we should get going," Lana slurred as she walked into a chair which she proceeded to apologise to.

"It's early girl, come on, one more hour or so!" Phoebe took a few unsteady steps towards and grabbed ahold of her.

The Eye Ball was a small joint, a long bar ran alongside the far wall and the ceilings were low, keeping the air hot and heavy. A small dance-floor illuminated by a silver disco ball was located to one side of the bar and a few tables were set up on the opposite side. Everyone was standing as they shouted to one another over the pulsing music, which consisted of underground electronica and rock that Lana had never heard before. The drinks were all unique to the bar, boasting 'Screaming Gore-fests' and 'Werewolf Lips', she got the sense that this bar only catered to a niche market. This was further reinforced by the crowd of eccentric clientele who shamelessly paraded around in vintage fashion and numerous pierced body parts. They chewed gum as they drank and danced with a combination of side-steps and arm flailing. Lana was grateful enough to be drunk enough to not be too self conscious. This wouldn't have been the sort of place she would have visited on her own, and though she was accustomed to frequenting many different types of bars and restaurants with her clients, she felt more comfortable in a place like Miami's.

"I'm pretty beat," Lana said, holding on to the wall for support, "I'll make my way home, you can stay."

"No way, I'm not letting you leave on your own!" Phoebe shouted as a heavy dance track blared over the speakers. "You're staying at mine tonight."

Lana watched Phoebe finish off the rest of her drink and motioned for her to get her jacket.

The air outside was cold and the two girls exhaled small clouds of breath which floated and vanished in front of them as they linked arms to cross a road. The streets were quiet despite the occasional passing car.

"Thanks for tonight," Lana said slowly.

"Any time, Lanny," Phoebe replied, punctuating the last word with a hiccup.

"Are you sure you don't mind me staying the night?"

"Of course not, it'll be like the old days!" Phoebe slurred and chuckled.

They continued to make their way down the narrow street, the streetlights flickered occasionally overhead and Lana was suddenly overcome with the sensation that she was being watched. She glanced around and squinted in an attempt to gain some focus on her surroundings.

"What's wrong?" Phoebe asked.

"I'm not sure," Lana replied as she turned her head in the other direction, "I just got the feeling that we're being watched."

Phoebe had a quick look around and returned eye contact with Lana, "I think you may have had way too many Werewolf Lips."

Lana giggled and nodded loosely.

They arrived at Phoebe's block and made their way to the elevator, as they stepped inside and watched the doors begin to close, Lana caught a glimpse of a figure stood at the entrance to the building. She could have sworn she saw his eyes glow as he took a step in their direction. The doors made a beep as they closed completely and the carriage began to rise.

"Did you see that?" Lana gasped, she had backed up against the wall, fear flickered in her eyes.

"What? What's wrong Lanny?" Phoebe placed a hand on her shoulder.

"I saw someone." She panted, "there was someone at the entrance of the lobby, watching us. I think he's following me. It looked as though he was coming towards us."

"Hey, calm down, there was no-one there. We've just had a little too much to drink, that's all," Phoebe gently shook her shoulder. "I promise, everything's okay. Derek's home so you'll feel safe when we get inside. Nothing's gonna happen."

"There was someone there. I'm not seeing things."

"Alright, alright, maybe someone was there but they could've just been returning home. It's fine."

The elevator reached the tenth floor and the two girls walked out into the hallway with trepidation. Though Phoebe hadn't seen anyone, Lana's reaction had made her feel uneasy - she had never seen her friend behave like that before.

The hallway was empty and Phoebe reached into her purse to get her keys. They continued down the corridor and stopped outside Phoebe's apartment. Lana had frantically looked behind her the entire time to make sure they weren't being followed, she was sure she could hear footsteps but kept quiet as she sensed that she had scared her friend and she needed her to stay calm incase something were to happen. Phoebe quickly unlocked the door and the two girls stumbled inside. A sense of relief washed over Lana but she could not shake the feeling that someone was following her and she concluded that the incidents that occurred the previous day were far from being coincidental.

Chapter Eight

It was clear where Cemetery Road had gained its name. Tyler stood at the entrance to a large graveyard that hadn't been tended to in quite some time. In the distance he could see an old church though it resembled a disused relic with its crumbling walls covered with creeping ivy and an array of overgrown thistle bushes surrounding it. Tombstones jutted out of the ground in numerous directions, some webbed in deep green moss, others with cracked faces or corners completely weathered away from the rain. The cemetery was surrounded by a wrought iron fence that had been painted black and stood at approximately three feet high. The gate to the entrance had been chained and padlocked, further confirming Tyler's suspicions that the church was no longer in use.

He cast his eyes over the remaining surroundings. Opposite to the cemetery was a large open field and a narrow road that stretched into the distance on both sides. Large oak trees lined either side of the road blocking the view of any potential residences. *Tara had been right in her description of the area,* Tyler thought, though Edenville appeared to be more like a remote hamlet than it did a small town and unlike any place Tara would willingly inhabit. The Tara he had grown up with had always been drawn to places where there was bustling life and people. Edenville had so far presented only the opposite. Tyler pulled the letter out of his backpack and scanned the address, he remembered it was house number Fifty One but he wanted to refer to the note to confirm his memory. He decided to follow the road down to his left as he had observed the street sign a little bit further down assuming it would lead him straight to the residential area. As he walked along the curvature of the road, he was overcome by the sheer stillness of the area. There was no birdsong, nor the quiet whistle of a slight breeze to remind him of any form of life. It was almost as though he had entered a remote vacuum where nothing went in and nothing came out. This was a distinct contrast to the life he was used to in London and it made him feel incredibly uneasy. Even his footsteps seemed to be muted with each step he took. Tyler came to a bend in the road and the residences eventually came into view.

He had never seen a street quite like it. There only appeared to be three detached houses on one side and five on the other. In the distance, further expanses of fields could be seen and beckoning hills loomed on the horizon casting a gloomy shadow over the land. Despite the fact that Tyler had located an area where there should be life, the street still appeared to be eerily quiet. There were no retired husbands out mowing the lawns or tending to their gardens. Not a single car could be seen in the driveways, and yet the houses appeared immaculate. Though they retained the features of homes that may have been stood for a century or so, not a tile or wood panel was out of place. The paintwork on each of the buildings was flawless and the bricks, though somewhat faded in places, looked healthy and unaffected by the ever-changing British weather. Tyler had presumed there would be more residences what with Tara living at house number Fifty One but on closer inspection, the house numbers appeared to be quite erratic. The first one was numbered, One Nine Five, the second one was Twenty Two. As he passed the houses, there appeared to be no life inside. Though he could observe the dark silhouettes of furniture through the windows, the homes seemed to be nothing but empty husks of lives that had now passed on.

Tara had always been so full of life and energy that Tyler was struggled to believe that she would be happy living in an area quite like Edenville. As he approached the last house, numbered Fifty One, he was overcome the sensation that he had made a mistake. He had felt all along that there was something not quite right with the letter he had received. *Maybe there had been another pair of siblings who shared their names and this letter had ended up at his address in error,* he considered but shook off the ludicrous thought almost immediately.

He paused in the driveway and looked up at the two storey house. It too, matched the other homes and looked to be in pristine condition. Though the house itself was made of brick, the windows and doors were framed with wood panelling that had been painted white. Intricate carvings of vines and blossoming flowers decorated the corners of the panels and Tyler was amazed at the detail that had gone into each piece. A wide open porch led to the front entrance and a medium sized garden bloomed with a magnificent array of colour directly in front of it. A sturdy oak tree overshadowed one side of the house and a small fence ran all around the outskirts. Even though it had been almost a decade since he last saw her, Tyler couldn't comprehend how much his sister had changed now that she was residing in a house like the one he currently gazed up at in amazement.

Wonder and confusion swam around in Tyler's body as he pushed open the front gate and walked up the garden path. The house appeared to grow as he made his way to the front door which loomied over him like one of the tombstones he had observed earlier on in the cemetery. A mixture of excitement and anxiety began to intermingle with his earlier emotions. He was moments away from reconnecting with his best friend - the sister that been nothing but supportive and defended him at whatever cost. He knew he was forever in debt to her and as he used the door knocker to announce his arrival, he began to feel foolish about his decision to take his life. Though that image of the housewife hanging over the dining room table would never leave his mind, he was not sure he could leave his sister with a similar parting image. This was the first spark of life he had felt in a while. He had first sensed this spark when he had met Geoff on his journey to Edenville, but now as he stood in front of this strangely quaint house, he felt further ignited with a sense of relief. Relief that he hadn't followed through with his plan and though he knew he shouldn't speak ill of the dead, he cursed the hanging housewife for providing him with the idea of that fatal option. The sound of a key in a lock rattled on the other side of the door and Tyler felt a smile begin to stretch across his face. He was merely seconds away from the reunion. This however, quickly vanished the very moment the door was pulled open.

*

Lana had woken before everyone else. Even though she had been fairly intoxicated, she had been unable to sleep. The image of the figure at the entrance to the building stuck with her and she could not shake the feeling that she was being targeted. As she lay on the sofa, listening to Phoebe's heavy breathing come from the floor beside her, she attempted to understand what it was that she had done to provoke the undesired attention. She thought back to meeting up with a client a few nights earlier, an older married gentleman called Ricardo. He was a regular client and he only ever treated her well. Sometimes they would go to a restaurant out of town, sometimes a cinema or a gallery. He would make a two hour journey from his hometown out of fear of being noticed by someone who knew either him or his wife. Their meetings were often in the day time and they rarely ever ended sexually. Lana charged her encounters based on the level of intimacy. Dates and companionship were the cheaper options and she found that she enjoyed the company of some of the men that would opt to take her out and spend time talking and getting to know her. She had encountered a few creeps along the way and this was a problem due to her working independently - there was no thorough screening process. Her conditions were that that had to initially meet in a public place, after that, Lana would either agree or disagree to the encounter going any further. Most of the time, there were no problems but some of the men had put on a good performance with their initial meeting, yet behind closed doors turned into monsters. Though she had never been in a position where she feared for her life, she had occasionally found herself tending to cuts and bruises. Lana didn't like to use the word 'rape' but sometimes things had gone a little too far out of her comfort zone and her pleas to stop had been ignored. She knew there were often blurred boundaries in her chosen line of work and had often considered going through a private agency but she couldn't justify their percentages.

Ricardo, despite his acts of adultery was a good man. He spoke to her with respect and when things became more intense he didn't want to 'fuck' her like the other men, he instead wanted to 'make love'. He paid generously and always left her a small gift - chocolates, roses, a personal letter (unsigned). She couldn't imagine that Ricardo would be responsible for having someone torment her. The only conclusion she could come to was that perhaps his wife had discovered his little secret and this was her way of exacting revenge.

Lana boiled the kettle and made an instant coffee, she took a sip and looked out of the kitchen window. The view from Phoebe's apartment didn't provide as much of a flattering perspective of the city as her apartment did.

Another apartment complex blocked any view of the city, its grimy walls and unwashed windows made Lana feel like she needed to take a shower. She finished her coffee and checked on Phoebe who had still not moved from her position. She made her way to the bathroom and switched the shower on. Lana locked the door in case she woke Derek and he attempted to come into the bathroom mistaking her for Phoebe. She waited a few moments for the room to grow steamy and hot and prepared herself to wash away any residual fear. A hot shower had solved many problems for her over the years. There was something cleansing about turning the heat up slightly higher than bearable and allowing it to transform her pale skin to a bright shade of scarlet upon contact. Sometimes she would force herself to stay under the water flow until she would feel as though she was about to pass out from the heat. She'd allow the extreme burning sensation to penetrate her skin and cause her body to vibrate slightly, at that moment she would switch the shower off. Those first moments of relief from the pain made her feel like she was reborn - she was liberated and forgiven of any former sins. She could regress to becoming a little girl once again if only momentarily. As the room began to fill with the steam, she became aware of a dark shadow in the corner by the faucet. Lana immediately froze as she tried to understand what it was. She wanted to switch the shower off to clear the steam but that meant approaching the dark shape. To her, it looked like a man crouching down, as though awaiting to pounce. Her next instinct was to call for help but that would only make the intruder aware that she had spotted him. Trying not to make any fast movements, she took a few steps backwards until her back made contact with the bathroom door. Keeping her eyes on the dark shadow-like object, she clumsily felt around for the handle, as she found it, she slowly pulled it down and pushed the door open. The shape remained motionless, *has he seen me?*

What is he waiting for? She began to question what motive had driven this monster to hide in the bathroom. As she pushed the door open a little further, the steam began to clear and Lana waited a moment to see if she could catch a glimpse of who was waiting for her. It was moments like these that she wished she was more like Phoebe. Her friend would have stormed over there with no hesitation and kicked the bastard clear in the face. As much as she wanted to drum up that form of courage, she couldn't bring herself to take a step closer. It was as the steam began to evaporate further that Lana began to see the shadow in more detail. It certainly matched the size and shape of a man crouched in the corner yet the thing she had feared was nothing more than an overflowing clothes hamper. Lana exhaled deeply and placed a hand over her mouth to stifle her desire to laugh at her foolishness.

Chapter Nine

Her hair was grey and it cascaded past her shoulders in long flowing wisps and curls. A pair of antique-style reading glasses hung loosely around her neck and an amethyst-coloured dress that covered her arms and ankles clung to her slender frame. Deep permanent creases lined her face like an intricate map of meandering rivers and estuaries. She looked at Tyler with emerald green eyes which widened in surprise after a few moments of opening up the front door.

"I'm sorry, I'm looking for Tara Hamilton, does she live-"

Before Tyler could finish his sentence, the woman had grabbed hold of him and wrapped both of her bone-like arms around him tightly, he caught a scent of her earthy perfume. Nothing about this woman seemed familiar.

"Tye! Is that really you? My God!" She pulled him in closer.

Tyler struggled to speak with her slightly damp hair clinging to his lips, "sorry, do I know you?" he asked blowing the strands out of his mouth.

The woman pulled back, the light behind her eyes appeared to fade and she let her hands drop by her side.

"I guess not," she answered solemnly.

"I got a letter from my sister, she mentioned that she was living here. I presumed she was living alone. Is she home?" Tyler couldn't understand why Tara would be living with an older lady and a number of different scenarios began to play out in his mind.

"No, I'm sorry, I-I don't know of an erm.. a Tara? She might've lived here maybe... at some point... but not anymore," the old lady replied, she was suddenly unable to make eye contact with him.

"How did you know my name?" Tyler asked.

The old lady didn't reply.

"When I was introducing myself, you said my name. Tye. How did you know that?"

He watched as she seemed to squirm under the weight of the question, she stepped from one foot to the other. It was a tic that Tara used to display if she was lying of nervous about something.

"You must've said it - y'know before you asked me, you said, 'my name's Tyler' that's what you did-"

"No, I definitely didn't mention my name, and you called me 'Tye'. There's only a few people that call me that," Tyler replied, he was growing considerably anxious. He looked past the woman and into the hallway. Hung on the far wall was a photograph and he immediately recognised it, it was a picture of Tara and himself in their local pub on the day of his graduation. Tara had always loved that photograph and would put it on full display in every home she had ever lived in, she claimed it was one of the proudest moments of her life - seeing her baby brother graduate. Something she, herself had failed to do.

"Where is my sister?" Tyler didn't recognise the change of tone in his voice at that moment but his stern delivery seemed to have an impact and the old lady finally made eye contact with him.

"W-what?"

"You heard me. Where is she? Tara!" He shouted past the woman and into the house, wondering if Tara was inside. *Was she being kept prisoner by this woman? Was that the real reason she had sent the letter?*

"There's no Tara living here, you have the wrong address. I'm sorry, you'll have to leave here now," her voice began to shake as she backed up inside the hallway, she started to close the door and Tyler quickly used his foot to prevent it from closing.

"Look lady, I'll be calling the police if you don't tell me where she is," Tyler moved his face closer to hers and tried to push the door open. He glanced back at the graduation photograph to confirm that it was indeed, a picture of himself and Tara.

"No, don't call the police, please don't do that," she begged.

"Just tell me where she is, that's all I ask," Tyler softened his tone slightly as he noticed genuine fear the woman's face.

"I'm telling you the truth, there's no Tara living here. Maybe she lived here before I did-"

"No." Tyler interrupted her.

"I said, you have the wrong address," she repeated.

"Well then explain to me why you knew my name?"

"I told you, it was the first thing you said."

"Even if that was true, I never introduce myself as Tye, only my close friends call me that."

The lady went quiet again.

"And also, can you explain that picture you have in your hallway, that one of me and my sister?"

Tyler watched the old lady slowly rotate her head to look down the hallway at the picture, she lowered her head as she turned back to him.

He pulled his phone out of his pocket.

"That's it, no more of this bullshit, I'm getting the police involved right now," he unlocked his phone and began to dial nine-nine-nine.

"No! Please! Don't do that!"

Tyler held his finger over the button to connect the call.

"Tye, it's me. It's Tara. I'm Tara. Don't call the police, I will explain. everything, just don't make that call."

Tyler looked up at the face that was claiming to be his sister. For the first time since her initial reaction when she saw him, she looked to be projecting a genuinely sincere response. She held her wrinkled hand over the phone, it was a hand he did not recognise.

"You should come inside," she said as she pulled the door open wider to allow him in.

*

Lana arrived home shortly after Phoebe and Derek had cooked her a large breakfast. They spent the remainder of the morning drinking coffee and trying to recall the events of the previous night. Lana had decided to keep the bathroom incident to herself, she felt foolish enough scaring herself the way she did and didn't want to extend the embarrassment any further. It made her feel slightly better about the situation and less paranoid that someone was intent on following her every move. As she walked from phoebe's apartment to hers, she noticed the air had changed quite dramatically - it was fresh and the skies were white, it appeared that snow was on the way.

As she passed Bobby in the lobby of her building, he told her that he'd reviewed all the footage from yesterday afternoon but found nothing of the strange man who had tried to enter her apartment. He reassured her that he was going to be extra vigilant and asked that if she had any suspicions to ring down to the front desk immediately. She was grateful for his assistance, his concern reminded her that some people still managed to retain a genuine sense of compassion for others.

She unlocked her apartment, feeling a little uneasy as she recalled the last time she had been there was when the incident had taken place. Though she may have been accustomed to a stranger's touch, she wasn't familiar with a stranger attempting to enter her home without her permission. She locked the door as she stepped inside and securely placed the chain in position. A draught blew through the hallway and Lana realised she had left the window open in the living room. She wrapped her arms around her torso to try and block out some of the chill as she made her way through the apartment. She entered the main room and observed the curtains billowing like two phantoms guarding the large window, she pulled at the handle and slammed it shut. The room was deathly cold so she proceeded to switch the heating dial to maximum and turned the television on to provide some background noise. Lana was not sure she could handle too much silence in that moment. In an attempt to put her mind at ease, she walked from room to room checking that she was in fact alone and free of any home invaders. She was attempting to put the strange incident to the back of her mind but she still wanted to be slightly more cautious. Bobby's reassurance had helped her considerably and she momentarily debated asking Phoebe to come over to stay the night so she at least wasn't alone. She shook her head to dismiss the idea, *I'm not going to let one weirdo unsettle me,* she thought.

Whilst Lana had walked home, she had contemplated whether she should give Cassandra's Emporium one more attempt. It was like Phoebe had said, the people that frequented these places were not being forced to do anything that they didn't want. They were not being made to hand over their money with a pistol pointed to their head, it was all completely and utterly voluntarily. Though she felt far from qualified, Lana considered that the worst that could happen would be that wasn't able to provide the necessary closure that someone was potentially searching for. The only thing they would lose perhaps is a considerable amount of their earnings. *But that's their choice,* she told herself.

Lana made herself a pot of tea and loaded up the site, she logged in once again and decided to embellish her profile slightly. She liked how her name was inspired by the word 'oracle' and she considered that it sounded the right amount of mysterious as it did exotic. She even conjured up an adventurous backstory in her mind, one that involved ominous ancestors who made a living by reading people's fortunes as part of a travelling circus. Their gift was passed on to the first-born females of each generation and with careful tuition and practice, they would become some of the greatest fortune tellers that the world had never known. She smiled slightly at her creative fluffing and used some of this feigned history as part of her profile. Once she had completed her profile she sat back, sipped on her cup of tea and watched the activity in the main chatroom unfold.

USER-5692: My husband recently passed away, I just need to know that he's at peace now. Help please?

USER-Dark_Swan_80: Thnkn of quttn my jb, nd sum advce

PSYCHIC_MEL: hi USER-5692 sorry to hear of your loss, I often make contact with the recently deceased, especially if they have something to say and pass on to their loved ones. I'm getting a strong connection with your message, if you would like a reading, please Direct Message me. Click on my name and follow the instructions. Peace be with you.

USER-256: Feeling pretty low tonight...................

USER-Robby1970: Stopping by to say thank you to Martha, your reading from Monday was spot on. I just wanted you to know that I've taken your advice and I have no doubt that I'm about to embark on an incredible journey. You're an angel. Thank you, thank you, thank you x

Mystical-Misty-xo: Hello USER-Black_Swan_80 your msg really spoke out to me, I have gr8 pre-cognitive abilities and I can give you some in depth advice on your question. DM for a reading.

PSYCHIC_MEL: USER-256, I understand your feelings, if it helps to know that I am here and will try and help you as best as I can. We can be good listeners as well as offering readings. Peace be with you.

USER-7981: FUCKING SHIT!!!! DONT BELIEVE THESE STUPID CUNTS! ALL LIES! ALL OF IT!!!!!! WASTE OF MONEY!!!!

USER-256: I'm not sure I can carry on….

ADMIN: USER-7981 HAS BEEN BLOCKED DUE TO BREAKING THE SITE'S TERMS AND CONDITIONS. POLITE REMINDER, PLEASE REFRAIN FROM USING BAD LANGUAGE AND ABUSIVE TERMS. CASSANDRA'S EMPORIUM IS A PLACE OF LOVE AND CONNECTEDNESS AND WE DO NOT TOLERATE NEGATIVE COMMENTS.

The chatroom scrolled on with further comments, all of which carried a similar tone. Lana held her fingers over the keyboard thinking of how to word a response to one of these users but the words wouldn't come to her. She noticed that most of the psychics would copy and paste their messages and seem to hammer them out to each new user. Some were careful not to be too obvious but she was surprised at the desperation in an attempt to fish for a customer, their hope that one of them would take the bait and reply with a direct message was painstakingly clear. Lana wasn't sure she could sell herself out so readily and as she further contemplated whether or not she was wanted to drop her name into the chatroom ocean, the laptop beeped.

NEW MESSAGE.

Lana recalled how this had happened the first time she had logged on but she was to afraid to open it.

"Okay, let's try this," she said aloud to herself and clicked on the pop up box.

NEW MESSAGE FROM: BlackButterfly

Hi Orla, how are you?

Lana hadn't expected to receive such an open message and her first inclination was that the message was a form of junk mail. However, from what she understood about the site, there was a basic charge for each message sent to a psychic so whoever 'BlackButterfly' was, they had just parted with fifty cents to ask her how she was.

Lana quickly typed a response.

Psychic_Orla: Hi BlackButterfly, I am very well thank you for asking. How are you? How can I help you today?

Lana waited anxiously as she saw the message icon indicate, *'the user is writing a message... please wait.'*

BlackButterfly: Thank you, yes I am very well. Have you had a good day?

Lana was baffled, she was half expecting for BlackButterfly to start to ask for a reading but instead, she seemed to be more interested in how she was doing.

Psychic_Orla: I've had a very good day so far.
How has your day been? Would you like a reading?

There was a slight pause before Lana saw that the user was typing a response to her. This was far from what she had been expecting but proved to be relatively easy. So far she had made fifty cents from two quick-fire messages, fifty percent went to Cassandra and the site administrators but the rest went directly to her. Lana was to charge extra for any reading and this could be any amount, the only condition was that it had to be mutually agreed before the reading could commence. It was in the psychics best interest to keep full transcripts of every message and transaction should there be any disagreements further down the line. Cassandra's team had access to all messages and these were saved on their servers if a lawsuit or further action was threatened. It seemed that they knew exactly what they were doing and the whole process appeared to be water-tight.

BlackButterfly: Thank you. I don't have much time
so I was wondering if I could just cut to the chase
and please ask that you help me?

Lana suddenly felt anxious, *what sort of help was BlackButterfly looking for?* From the username, she imagined a young teenage girl, bullied at school for being different and unable to talk to anyone unless anonymously through a Psychic chatroom. Lana suddenly felt nervous, she wasn't a qualified counsellor, how was she able to help someone with problems that didn't involve her supposedly connecting with the dead or telling someone to follow their gut instinct. On the other hand, she would feel awful turning down someone's plea for help, she couldn't just ignore the request.

Psychic_Orla: Sure, how can I help?

Lana watched as the message box informed her that her recipient was typing a message. She wondered what she was going to ask for. Just before BlackButterfly's message appeared, another message flashed up on screen.

YOUR BATTERY IS LOW. SYSTEM GOING INTO STANDBY MODE TO RESERVE POWER.

The laptop screen went black.

"No!" Lana shouted, she quickly scanned the room for the power lead, *why did I not think to connect to the power mains?* She cursed herself. "Fuck, fuck, fuck!"

Lana scrambled around the living room, lifting up the sofa cushions and throwing them on the floor, only to find an amass of crumbs and loose change. She flicked through the magazine stand to see if she had placed it in there.

Nothing.

This happened frequently and she knew that she would only have a couple of minutes before the power would cut out completely, this would mean losing the chat with BlackButterfly until she could power up the laptop again. Her heart pounded, she didn't quite understand why she felt so responsible for this particular stranger. *She chose me,* she thought. *Out of all the other psychics, she picked me. I can't let her down, not now.* Lana ran out of the living room and into her bedroom, she flung back the bedcovers and scanned under the bed to no avail.

"Where the fuck is it?"

The intensity of her heart rate made her feel as though she was about to vomit. She pulled open the bedside cabinet drawers and rummaged through the bottles of lotions, perfumes and hair products, yet no power cord was to be found. She tried to remember where she had it last, but just as much as she tried to squeeze the memory out of her brain, it became harder and harder to access. She stood in the doorway and scanned the room once more, and then she remembered. She had used her laptop to listen to music whilst she was in the bath, she had plugged it in to the electrical outlet in the hallway, Her feet pounded along the floorboards as she ran to the bathroom and there, right in the corner by the scales was the power cord, loosely bundled together.

"Darn it!"

She charged over and scooped it up and ran back to the living room. The power light was still flashing on the keyboard, *yes,* she thought, *there's still time.* She plugged the cord in and grabbed the other outlet and slotted it into the laptop jack. The moment it clicked into place, the power light flashed off.

"What? No-"

She stared at the screen for a moment, wishing it back to life.

"Come on, come on, come on-" she muttered under her breath, she was resisting the urge to touch any of the keys unless they shut the computer off entirely. After a few moments, the laptop made a humming noise, her heart began to pound - it was coming back to life!

"Please, please still be there-" she prayed quietly under her breath.

Suddenly the screen flashed with the logo of the computer brand - it had restarted. Lana exhaled sharply realising that she had lost her conversation with BlackButterfly completely.

Chapter Ten

"Take a seat. Can I get you a drink?"

Tyler had done as much as possible to steady himself as he walked into this strange woman's house - this woman who had so far claimed to be his sister. This woman, who bore not even a single physical resemblance to Tara, who wore clothes that she wouldn't have been seen dead in. There was an upper-class twang in her words that sounded nothing like Tara's southern colloquialisms. In fact, the only small similarity were some of her mannerisms - the way she stepped from foot to foot when he had called her out on the lie from earlier on or the way she would gesture with her hands as she spoke. There was certainly something uncanny about this woman's behaviour but he couldn't see anything of Tara in her physical appearance. An intense dizzy spell began as he had stepped inside her home. There was an unusual atmosphere contained within those walls, as though the altitude had suddenly switched but he knew that sort of phenomena was impossible. Tyler sensed that something was most certainly not as it seemed and he wondered if the building itself had picked up on his growing apprehension. As he passed the photograph that hung on display at the end of the hallway, he lightly touched it to make sure that it was indeed real. The cool glass on his fingertips confirmed that it was most definitely not a mirage. Within that frame which was decorated with elaborate swirls and scrolls was a memory captured of himself and Tara - their bond resonated undeniable and unscathed. There was no way of telling that fate would inevitably separate them years later, the look in their eyes suggested they were to be friends until the end.

The house itself contained nothing that would be deemed unusual. No piles of bones in the corners of the rooms, no blood stains on the walls, although this did little to settle Tyler's nerves. The decorating emulated the exterior, it was impeccable - as though it had only been finished a few moments before Tyler had knocked on the door. The wallpaper patterns matched up perfectly, the paintwork was pristine - not a drop out of place. The furniture, though vintage in style was in great condition. As the woman had led him into the living room, he noted its more than accommodating size - a large bay window overlooked the back garden, the grass seemed to flourish with a vibrant green glow and the potted plants stretched up to the sun almost as if they were feverishly worshipping the giant ball of fire in the sky. The room though quite large was made to feel more cosy and homely with a coffee table that presented numerous small knick-knacks and ornaments, a newspaper, a magnifying glass, a paperback novel - nothing out of the ordinary. A wood-stained bureau stood against one wall, it was filled with decorative cutlery and a collection of varying sized candlestick holders. In the centre of the room was a large floral-patterned sofa and two sturdy armchairs with a matching design placed at precise right-angles around the coffee table.

The woman gestured for Tyler to take a seat on the two-seater sofa.

"Just a water please," he answered.

"Be back in just a moment," she replied as she swiftly left the room.

Tyler further scanned the room looking for more information as to who this woman really was. There were no more photographs to provide a hint of any other family members or friends. He noted that this was a typical trait of Tara, she had only ever displayed that one particular memory of the two of them together on his graduation day. Tyler placed both hands down beside him on the sofa to steady himself, his head was still spinning. Attempting to try to comprehend what was going on was beginning to take its toll so he had to remind himself to take a deep breath and hear this crazy woman out. He wanted to see how she could explain to him that she was his sister and better yet, he wanted to know where Tara was. *Maybe she has one of those mental disorders?* Tyler thought, *one of those multiple personality syndromes perhaps?* He didn't know much about those sort of conditions but he pondered the idea that if it came to light that this woman was indeed displaying the pre-requisites for a mental health condition, he wasn't sure how he should then proceed to handle the situation. *Just listen to what she has to say,* he told himself before taking another deep breath.

"Here you go," the woman returned with a large glass beaker filled with water, she held a steaming mug in her other hand.

She carefully took a seat on one of the armchairs, a big smile was painted across her face. "Firstly let me just say, Tye, you look great and I've missed you so much. I couldn't more happier to see you. I'm just sorry-" her voice trailed off.

Tyler was still baffled at her consistent pretence of pretending to know and share a history with him.

"I have no idea who you are," he started, "are you a friend of my sister or somethin'?"

The woman slowly shook her head.

"I just don't understand what's going on here."

"I know this must be really confusing for you," she said sorrowfully.

"Too fuckin' right," Tyler muttered under his breath.

"I can't tell you too much Tye but I am okay, I promise.," the woman paused and nibbled her bottom lip before continuing to speak, "I'm fine but I have to ask you to leave here and pretend that none of this happened, okay?"

"What? No way! You promised me an explanation. How can you ask me to pretend that nothing's going on when it clearly is?" he could feel a red heat forming in the skin on his face, "all I need to do is call the police and have them question you to find out where my sister is."

"Tye, please-"

"Stop fuckin' callin' me that!" He blurted out.

The woman flinched slightly at his outburst.

"I'm sorry," she said, "I am Tara though, I know how crazy this all seems but I assure you it's me but I need you not to draw any attention to me being here. Please, I beg you. I can't risk-" she stopped herself.

"You can't risk what? Someone finding out that you've kidnapped my sister, or worse that-that you killed her! Is that it? Have you murdered her?" Tyler began to rise from his seat, he started to clench and unclench his fists in succession.

"No! Not at all! Tye, it's me, it's Tara, I can prove to you-"

"Well then prove it, tell me something that only Tara and I would know, " Tyler demanded, he remained standing over her.

The woman shifted uncomfortably in her seat, "okay," she said softly.

A strange silence descended upon the room and Tyler wondered what crazy story she was going to come up with next.

"You were about six years old, I was about fourteen. Mum was having one of those parties she used to host every other night. We were so sick of it. Having to go to school the next day with only a couple hours of sleep, the kids pickin' on us because of the bags under our eyes and not being able to concentrate in class. We were so sick of it. Coming home to find her off her face, strangers snorting or shooting up in various rooms of the house. We bought locks for our bedroom doors because we were terrified one of them was going to come into the room in the middle of the night and do somethin'. That bitch soon broke those locks right off the doors in one of her drunken rages."

Tyler couldn't believe what this woman was saying, everything so far had been accurate. However, Tara was not afraid of telling people how much of a mess their home life had been, many people were aware about their mother and her lifestyle. It wasn't something that couldn't be found out with a little questioning. Tyler, however, was intrigued to see what else she had to say. He knew that there were things that only Tara would know, things that she most definitely would not share with anyone else apart from him, and him alone. Those secrets were to stay between them for as long as they lived.

"There was one night," she continued, "we barricaded ourselves in my room. I had propped a chair up against the door, y'know the one I used to use as a make-up table, and we pretended we were playing hide and seek or something. I was so scared for you. I didn't want anything to happen and I was so angry at her for tormenting us the way she did. She'd tell us how much she wished she had aborted us and that having children ruined her life. I hated her and I felt so protective of you." The woman paused, tears had formed in her eyes but Tyler could see that she was fighting them off. "See, I always said I would never cry for her and I won't," she took another deep breath, "I won't," she repeated.

The anger that had raged through Tyler earlier on had ceased, the blood pumped around his body in a slightly different manner this time - he was beginning to feel apprehensive about the direction of the story.

"That night - I had had enough. I was sick and tired of being scared all the time. I was fourteen years old and I felt like I was losing my mind. Some days were unbearable, just hearing her voice after a few drinks, seeing her with those men. It made me feel physically ill, but I never wanted to show you how it affected me. I wanted to be strong for you - you're my little brother. I wanted you to have a good life and be happy and not have to deal with all the shit she put us through. I can't remember the exact details of that evening. I don't know what it was that made her so angry but she charged up those stairs and straight to my room, I remember my heart was in my mouth. I thought she was going to kill us and I knew I had to protect you. I had to protect us. So that moment she broke through my door, I charged right at her. I didn't have any intentions, I just wanted to stop her from hurting us, but I also knew that right outside my door was the staircase. And at that moment my hands came into contact with her, I knew I could not stop pushing, and I didn't. She was at the top of the stairs, facing me, and her eyes - God, she looked terrified and sometimes when I think of her face in that moment, I wonder if she was sorry. That if in those last few seconds, she truly understood what it was that she had done to us for all those years. But still I pushed and down she went. It was like watching a film in slow motion and as she hit that bottom step and her neck twisted the way it did, I knew the story would be that she had fallen. It just came into my head, I could tell people that she had gotten completely wasted, tried to climb the stairs and she fell, broke her neck and died in that moment," the woman took a long breath, she was replaying something behind her eyes. "I still don't know how I got away with it and I knew you had seen it all. I was so worried that you would tell the truth, but you never did. You played along with the story and we never spoke of it again, not until now. You protected me all this time," she paused, "all these years."

There was no way that Tara would have told anyone else that story, not at the cost it would have come at. Tyler had kept that untold secret with him for so long and just as the woman had said, he had never mentioned the truth to a single soul. He hadn't wanted to open those wounds or risk losing his sister. All he had wanted was to move on and though their experiences in numerous different foster homes were not great, they had more of a life compared to living with their alcoholic mother. Tyler had often felt that he had helped Tara push their mother down the stairs, and in the rare moments when he recalled the incident, he imagined he was at the very top of the flight of stairs too and he had been the one to deliver that final push. Everything that the woman sat before him had said was true. There was not a single detail out of place and her conviction could not have be falsified or acted out. This woman; this strange woman whom Tyler had never in his life seen before was bizarrely and undoubtedly his beloved sister.

*

Lana had rebooted her computer and logged back into the chatroom a quickly as she could. The direct message had somehow been deleted and there was no trace of the conversation that had previously taken place with BlackButterfly. She sent out a message in the public chatroom in the hope that she would spot it.

'BlackButterfly, I was having a technical issue, please message again. Orla.'

The comment however, received no response and Lana spent the next two hours scrolling through all the list of active users to try and find someone named BlackButterfly only to no avail. She sent an email to the administrators to see if there was a way of contacting a previous user but they sent a standard response to say that it was a laborious task attempting to track and trace IP addresses and users as they frequently come and go and can change their profile name at any given time. Lana felt terrible, she had failed this one person who had reached out to her. She didn't know how old she was, where she lived or even if she was in fact, female. It occurred to her how strange it was that she felt so responsible for this stranger. For all she knew it could have been someone playing a prank but she was unable to shake the feeling that there was something more about the minimal interaction - a feeling that desperately clung to her and invaded her every thought.

Lana stayed up until the early hours, constantly checking the chatroom in case BlackButterfly returned. It was just before four a.m. when she gave up and retired to bed, burdened with the knowledge that she was unable to help a person that had reached out to her for help.

What sleep she managed to acquire was infiltrated with scrolling chatroom conversations, person after person asking for her help and Lana would try desperately to write to them but as soon as she hit 'send' to one reply another further twenty messages would come through. Her hands ached with the frantic typing and she could her the cries and sobs from the people who were reaching out to her, and she fretted, feeling as though she was failing every single one of them. Their pleas grew more and more desperate and intense and she looked down to observe her fingers transform into frost-ladened twigs. The ringing of her phone caused her to bolt upright in bed.

"Miss White, I hope I haven't disturbed you-" Lana recognised Bobby's voice instantly, "but when you get a moment, I'd like for you to come down and see me in the lobby at some point today."

"Hi Bobby, no - not a problem, I can do that, maybe in about half an hour or so?"

"That'll be fine, Miss White, please - no rush," Bobby soothed.

"Okay, I'll see you shortly,"

"Goodbye Miss White,"

"Bye."

Lana rubbed her eyes and stretched her arms above her head. The bedside clock read just after ten a.m. She felt completely exhausted, the last couple of days had depleted most of her energy levels. She took a quick shower and downed two coffees, one after the other. She logged back into Cassandra's and scoured her through the users list and checked her inbox only to find no new messages and more disappointingly, no BlackButterfly. She sighed and logged back out, she pulled on some clothes and made her way down to the lobby.

"Good morning Bobby," Lana smiled as she approached the front desk.

"Miss White," he replied politely as he tilted his head slightly towards her, "would you mind stepping around here with me?"

Lana followed his hand and came around to stand on the other side of the desk with Bobby. She watched as he typed away at the keyboards and pointed at one of the screens.

"Here, do you see?" Bobby asked.

Lana leaned in closely, she stared at the small monitor screen, she could make out a long aerial view of the hallway outside her apartment. The time stamp at the top of the screen read four eleven a.m. This was footage from just a few hours ago. Lana observed a dark shadow skulk across the hallway, the quality of the picture was not too clear but the black shape resembled that of a man.

"I know it might be difficult to see but does he look familiar? Were you expecting anyone?" Bobby enquired.

"It's difficult to say but he does have a similar build to the man who had tried to enter my apartment, but it's difficult to say for sure-" Lana was cut short as she watched the shadow approach her door. A chill ran through her body as he stayed fixed in position directly outside of her residence, apparently waiting for something. She shivered when she realised he was probably waiting for her.

"I don't mean to alarm you Miss White, but I have no idea how he got into the building at that time. I've been here at the desk for eighteen hours straight now and I've checked the footage of all the entrances and exits, but there is no sign of him getting in or leaving." Bobby explained, he touched a small dial by the side of the computer and sped the footage up demonstrating that the shadow remained directly outside Lana's door the whole time. He stopped it as the time stamp read eight, thirty-eight a.m. and Lana watched as the shadow walked down the rest of the corridor and turned out of sight around a corner at the far end.

"There's no cameras on that corner so I have no idea where he went after that," he said.

Lana's body had gone cold all over, she wrapped her arms around the front of her chest to prevent her from physically shaking.

"I don't understand," she whispered, "why I am I being targeted?"

"Miss White, I wouldn't worry. There's nothing here to suggest that any of this was premeditated and he didn't attempt to enter the apartment at any point. Granted, it's a little unusual but I promise I will be watching over this building, and your floor particularly like a hawk," Bobby reassured her.

"Thanks Bobby. I'm just not too sure I want to go back up to my apartment now-"

"He's not returned and this could just be a one-off but we won't take any risks. Do you have anyone you can call that could maybe stay with you or have you stay with them? I'll log this with the cops too."

"I can speak to a friend," Lana replied, she was struggling to avert her eyes from the screen. Part of her expected to see the shadow appear around the corner and begin to approach her apartment again, but whatever or whomever it was, stayed clearly out of sight.

"You're safe here Miss White so I'll leave it up to you, stay here or stay with a friend I'll be here to make sure nothing happens."

"Oh Bobby thank you. I'm not sure what I'll do. I will let you know," Lana said as she finally managed to pull her gaze away from the screen.

"No problem."

"Thanks again," she called as she began to make her way back to her freshly stalked apartment.

Chapter Eleven

Witnessing the strange woman tell the story that Tyler had so often privately revisited had been nothing short of surreal but he could see that she was reliving those very moments from behind her eyes. Though he had never directly spoken with Tara about what had happened, he had instinctively gone along with the story when he had been questioned numerous times from police and social workers. There had been no previous verbal agreement between them to suggest that he had to keep her secret but he knew there was no way that he could put the one person who had protected him for all those years in jeopardy. He never thought that it would get mentioned ever again, it had been the backbone of their unspoken bond for all those years. However, witnessing this confession delivered from a stranger was something he could only describe as deeply incongruent. He had spent a few moments in silence after she had explained the events of that night from her perspective, in an attempt to make sense of the bizarre situation. He knew there was no other way that this woman couldn't be Tara. She never would have mentioned a single word to anyone about the truth of what happened that night and as he attempted to uncurl this realisation, an insurmountable number of questions began to weigh heavy on him.

He decided to cut right to the chase.

"What's happened? Why do you look-" he paused, "this way?"

The woman shifted in her seat and looked down, her gaze became one with the carpet, embarking on an in-depth study of the tessellated pattern, her eyes appeared to trail and dance over each fine line and after a few moments Tyler began to wonder if she was ever going to answer his question.

"You understand why I'm struggling to make sense of this right?" he added.

She stayed silent.

"Tara had blue eyes, you have brown. She would be forty one years old now and not to cause any offence, you look to be in your late fifties. She was pretty liberal and messy, her house was never in order and yours is...is... well - it's cleaned to perfection. Tara had brunette hair and if she ever noticed a stray grey, she'd dye her entire head! Do you understand what I'm saying? You're nothing like her!" Tyler was struggling to maintain his composure.

"It is me Tye, I'm just older now. A lot has happened but you don't need to be alarmed. I am fine. I promise." She paused. "But you're gonna need to go now."

"I don't understand, it's like someone's transplanted my sister's memories into a completely different body. None of this makes sense and what's with the urgency for me to leave? Tara would never want me to leave?" Tyler began to feel the same seeds of doubt slowly start to sprout inside of him again. He was doubting the validity of what this woman was saying to him.

"I don't know what else I can do to prove to you Tye. It's me. Yes, I've changed, you've changed too. You chose to come out to me before anyone else, I introduced you to my friend Jake at that Halloween party Louisa held about fifteen years ago. You were the one who taught me how to drive, you bought me a lucky charm bracelet for my thirtieth birthday and I lost four of those charms that night we went out for drinks in the The Black Ram. We'd always sing Queen at karaoke and you had a weird obsession with Edgar Allan

Poe as a teenager-" she stopped speaking when she saw the tears in Tyler's eyes.

"It-It really is you? Isn't it?" He muttered between heavy breaths, "It's you, Tara?"

"It's me, Tye," she confirmed.

He stood up slowly and made his way over to the woman, she stood as he approached and they held each other. Tyler felt hot tears run down his face and she squeezed him tighter.

*

Upon returning to her apartment, Lana felt a dizzying sense of confusion and anxiety. The idea of a stranger waiting directly outside of her home, which was meant to be her supposed safe haven made her feel considerably on edge. As she took the elevator and ascended to her floor, she debated about packing up a suitcase and leaving for a few days but by the time the doors pulled open with a distinctly satisfying beep, she had talked herself out of that particular decision. She was not going to allow some creepy individual run her out of her own home. Lana had always taken pride in the fact that she was built of strong bone and thick skin and had no problem holding her own if needed - she was determined not to be made to feel afraid in the one place she considered home. Lana still made an effort to take some necessary precautions, so she proceeded to lock the front door and placed the chain in position when she returned. She then went to her bedroom and located a baseball bat that had belonged to an ex-boyfriend and took it into the living room with her. She rummaged through her kitchen drawer and pulled out the largest, sharpest knife she owned. This was carefully placed next to her as she booted up the computer and logged into Cassandra's Emporium. Her fingers instinctively clicked and scrolled as she searched through the users that were currently live in the chatroom. Her pupils flicked backwards and forwards looking for 'BlackButterfly' only to no avail. She sighed at the lack of results and as she sat staring at the screen cautiously toying with the kitchen knife beside her, she made a decision. Lana signed into the main chatroom and typed a message.

Psychic_Orla: Hi, looking to connect with BlackButterfly, if anyone knows her or has any information on how I can contact her, please get in touch.

She clicked 'send' and watch the message fall into the chatroom like a weighted feather and waited patiently for a response. She painstakingly observed the other messages flash across the screen and inevitably her message was quickly pushed out of view, it was as though any hope of finding more information disappeared with that message. In the same moment Lana reached to click on the 'log out' button, her screen beeped - someone had sent a private message. She held her breath as she opened it, silently praying that it was BlackButterfly.

Rita_White_Star190: Hi Psychic_Orla, I just saw your message in the chat room. How do you know BlackButterfly?

There was a slight sense of disappointment when Lana realised that it was another one of the online psychics that had messaged her but it instilled a small sense of hope, *perhaps she knows something?*

Psychic_Orla: Hi, she sent me a message last night, she needed help and I lost my connection with her. I'm worried that something has happened to her.

Lana watched as Rita began typing a response.

Rita_White_Star190: You're not the only one this person has reached out to. Whoever they are, I'm not sure they genuinely need our help.

Though Lana had a hint of suspicion about what BlackButterfly wanted, she still wanted to know what it was that was troubling her.

Psychic_Orla: What did she need help with?
Rita_White_Star190: You should have no contact with her.

Lana began to grow more frustrated at not receiving an answer.

Psychic_Orla: Yes, but why? What does she want?
Rita_White_Star190: You shouldn't be asking questions. I'm only trying to be nice.
Psychic_Orla: That sounds like a threat.

Rita_White_Star190: Listen, I'm only trying to warn you. There are people on here that genuinely need help. BlackButterfly is nothing but trouble. I mean it.

Psychic_Orla: I'm sorry but I can figure that out for myself.

Lana felt her blood begin to boil, she couldn't be sure if this other psychic had another intention.

Rita_White_Star190: Don't say I didn't warn you.

Psychic_Orla: Thanks for your warning but I will make my own decisions.

Rita_White_Star190: You'll end up dead. Like the others.

The message struck a chord with Lana. The bluntness of her words impacted her like an axe to the back of her skull.

] She immediately responded.

Psychic_Orla: What do you mean?

She waited for a response, but there was no indication that Rita was typing a message so she repeated the exacted same question.

Nothing.

Psychic_Orla: Hello? Are you still there?

Again, no answer.

Psychic_Orla: Hello? Are you still there?

Psychic_Orla: What do mean? There have been others?

Psychic_Orla: Hello?

YOUR RECIPIENT HAS LOGGED OUT

"What?" Lana shouted at her computer screen, "you've gotta be kiddin' me right?"

She stared at the messages that had been sent and shook her head. Her heart pounded in her chest and her mouth had gone dry. A horrifying thought struck her, *What if the stalker had something to do with BlackButterfly?* She logged out of Cassandra's Emporium and immediately picked up her phone.

*

The travelling and strange turn of events had taken their toll on Tyler. As soon as he had accepted the bizarre truth about Tara, he was immediately consumed with a feeling of weakness and fatigue. His head raged with a powerful headache and though he was in the company of his sister, he felt strange asking a face he didn't recognise if he was able to have a lie down for an hour or two. Her response came in two parts, the first began with a flash of excitement behind the dull eyes. The second part was presented with a frown and a drop of her head. It was almost as though she was battling with another persona that held the reigns to her true feelings. Tyler still found himself trying to put all the pieces together and there were a million more questions that he wanted to ask her but his body was going into shutdown mode. The idea of trying to locate a hotel or a bed and breakfast in the middle of this rural town was a feat he didn't think would be possible with his quickly deteriorating condition. After a momentarily deliberation, Tara agreed to let him have a lie down in the spare room. She led him upstairs with a walk that Tyler deemed to be very cautious. He took in as much of the house as possible, it was certainly very quaint - completely atypical of the sister he remembered. He found it difficult to adjust his view of Tara and to accept that perhaps she really had changed, not only in her physical appearance but personality-wise too. Thick carpets had been laid in all the rooms except for the hall and stairwell which consisted of deep brown oak coloured wood panelling. Framed portraits of various cottages and woodland filled some of the blank spaces on the floral wallpapered walls. As he climbed the stairs, there was one thing that stood out to Tyler - an oak-style crucifix hung at the exact midpoint of the stairwell. The finely detailed cross depicted an almost naked Jesus, his head bearing a crown of thorns, his eyeballs rolled back in a state of perpetual agony. Large nails had been driven through his palms and his feet, and the wound in the side of his abdomen - wide and gaping. The image had been carefully carved and then hand-painted - each drop of blood glistened red and that particular colour hadn't been used very sparingly. In fact, the entire image was gratuitous and bordered on offensive, he found it difficult to look at as he passed it. That wasn't the unusual part that had struck him as soon as he observed it - the reason it filled him with a cold shiver was knowing that Tara had always been a strict atheist. This had always been something she had strongly stood by and had had many a vehement argument with friends about the state of religion and her strong dislike for it. The old Tara would never have even entertained the idea of having any form of religious artefact in her home. This had been something that she was always certain of. Tyler made a mental note of the grotesque object, he was not going to mention it straight away but he was to store it in a part of his mind that was easily retrievable for when he needed it.

Tara had directed him to a small bedroom on the first landing. It was conveniently next to the bathroom and contained a small single bed, a window that looked out on to the back garden and an vintage-looking set of drawers. It was perfectly decorated in a similar pastel floral wallpaper and looked as though it had been sealed in Tupperware until the very moment she opened the door and advised Tyler to lie down. He thanked her and before he knew it, his eyelids clamped shut and he was consumed by sleep.

Tyler awoke with a heavy head, clear evidence that the rest was very much needed. He checked his watch, it was a little after two-thirty in the morning. A large luminescent moon lit up the room - the curtains had remained opened and Tyler immediately wondered if Tara had been in to check on him. He rubbed the sleep from his eyes, there had been a strange array of dreams that unfolded in the hours he had slept. Each one seemed to roll into the next creating an epic tale of surreal situations. The hanging housewife, his boss calling him into his office, a slow train ride through hell, his sister tearing her face away, the crucifix slowly inverting... As Tyler slowly allowed his eyes to adjust to the tiny room, the memories of the dreams quickly faded away until he could barely recall them. This came at a great relief. He wondered why Tara hadn't woken him. *Perhaps she had seen how much I needed a rest and didn't want to disturb me,* he thought. Sitting upright on the bed, he cast his eyes on the open door, the hallway was dark and he couldn't hear any sign of life. *She must be asleep.* In that moment, Tyler wondered if he should lie back down and sleep until morning but a creeping fear began to take hold. He couldn't be sure if it was due to the unknown surroundings or the fact that he was alone in a house with his sister who looked nothing like the sister he had grown up with. He tried to picture Tara's new face - how old she had looked, the slight arc in her back and the dry, grey hair. He knew that there was no way someone could age as much as that within eight years, it just didn't seem possible. Ignited by the fear, Tyler slowly put his feet to the floor and decided to have a little more of an extensive look around the house.

All the lights had been turned out, however the glow of the moon which had illuminated the room that Tyler had stayed in, spilled out on to the upstairs landing. There were four other doors, he knew one was the bathroom as it had been left open and he could see the ceramic faucet standing solemnly in front of him like an alter. All the other doors were closed and he didn't want to risk walking into Tara's room and waking her. He wanted to keep this trip as much of a private expedition as possible. He carefully made his way down the stairs, the floorboards appeared to creak with intense volume in the stillness and he flinched each time his foot made contact with one. Tyler passed the crucifix and made a conscious decision not to look at it in the eerie moonlight. He was trying to keep his heart rate steady and observing Jesus's agonised face would do quite the opposite. The silence that encased the house was almost unbearable and it made the trip down the stairs more nerve-wracking. He couldn't explain why he felt so on edge - being caught heading downstairs was easy enough to explain if Tara awoke but he couldn't shake the feeling that there was something a little more sinister under foot. Tyler ventured into the living room, only a few hours ago he had listened to his sister's confession, something he had never expect to hear from her. The empty seats looked forlorn in the darkness. He scanned the walls and looked through the bureau -

if he could find a letter or something with Tara's name, he would feel a little more at ease. Even better yet, if he could find anything that would explain the fact that she had an entirely new face - that would most definitely aid in wiping away every single doubt that had previously flooded his brain. However, the living room provided nothing that could set Tyler's mind at ease. He used the joining door to enter the dining room. A large rectangular table stood in the centre of the room, eight chairs had been carefully nestled beneath and eight place mats had been set at equal distances apart from each other. Tyler wondered if Tara regularly entertained guests but struggled to imagine that another seven people lived in the nearby vicinity. Once again, the wall was decorated with generic pictures of expansive countryside and little cottages with smoke billowing elegantly from their chimneys. Just like the living room, there was nothing in this room that would offer up any additional information so he stealthily navigated through the doorway, down the hallway, past his graduation picture and into the kitchen. He was immediately struck by how cold the room was, as though all the windows had been left open but he could see they were firmly closed. A large round table stood to one side and a counter top extended from beneath the window and out into the main section of the room, creating a breakfast bar. Like all the other rooms, it was immaculately presented and Tyler was reminded of a showroom house. Using his phone as a makeshift torch, he opened the drawers and cupboards and illuminated their interiors. Pots, pans, glasses and mugs had all been placed in perfect position and as he closed a drawer of utensils, he heard a noise. It was faint but it sounded like music. Tyler stood motionless trying to understand where the sound was coming from. He noticed another door in the kitchen. It was set in a small alcove and he realised this would have been the entry way to a basement. He approached the door and placed his ear against the wood.

The sound was a little more prominent.

Music.

Only a specific type of music.

This was the sort of music you would hear when you would open a music box and an enslaved ballerina would mechanically twirl to a tinny musical number that would gradually slow to a halt, beckoning to be wound up once more. Tyler could not recognise the tune, though it had a lullaby quality to it. Despite the low volume of the music he was certain that it was coming from behind the door.

He slowly grasped the doorknob and turned it.

Nothing.

The door was stuck stiff - it had been locked.

He tried once more in the hope that it required a little more force quite like the other doors in the old house. The door rattled slightly more but didn't budge confirming that it had indeed been locked. Tyler quickly exhaled in defeat as he observed a small keyhole just below the knob. He scanned the kitchen to see where the key might have been located, but as his eyes flicked from the walls to the counter, the music stopped abruptly.

He froze in position, he instinctively pulled his hand away from the knob and paused awaiting for any indication that his presence had been noticed.

Silence.

He waited a few more seconds before turning back and quickened his pace back to the hallway and up the stairs. He quickly lay down on his bed in an attempt to calm the heavy breath that was causing his chest to rise and fall in quick succession. He closed his eyes and he swore he heard a floorboard creak just outside of his room but he couldn't be sure of the exact location. He squeezed his eyes tight, hoping that he was successfully portraying a genuine act of being asleep. The silence descended on the room with perfect precision. All sound, except the thumping in his chest and the throbbing rush of blood in his ears was banished completely. He wondered if the woman who was claiming to be his sister was stood in his doorway, the door fixed wide open and her eyes watching him while he pretended to be asleep. The thought of a silent observer caused a chill to run through his body. He stayed in the same position all through the remainder of the dark hours, right until the sound of bird song could be heard just outside of the window.

Chapter Twelve

"You're staying with us tonight," Derek said as he gulped down a mouthful of beer, he slammed the pitcher down and wiped away an excess of foam from his mouth with the back of his hand.

"Yeah Lanny, you need to report this to the cops too, that asshole shouldn't be allowed to get away with terrorising women living on their own," Phoebe added.

Lana had nodded along with all the comments, but really her mind was elsewhere. After the conversation she had had with the other psychic had taken a sour turn, she couldn't help but wonder if what she had said was true and BlackButterfly was indeed nothing but trouble. Immediately after the exchange of messages, she had asked Phoebe and Derek to meet her at Miami's so she could assess their opinions about the situation. In actuality, she was grateful for the excuse to get out of her apartment and numb her snowballing thoughts with a cocktail. She wanted to do as much as possible to further distract herself from spiralling into conspiracy theories and the thought of being constantly watched. She was beginning to feel as though every thought was becoming consumed with BlackButterfly and what it was that she had wanted. Lana had even began to develop an image of her, not as a human but instead as a human-sized moth-like creature. She'd arrived in her consciousness as an entity cocooned in a wafter thin pod that wrapped up body like a makeshift coffin. She'd emerge each day, proceeding to stretch large dark wings and shake them loose before she would send out a plea online in the hope that she would be set free. Perhaps she was under a spell, cursed to live as a human sized butterfly, unable to venture out into the real world for fear of being rejected or pinned up in a Natural History Museum. Destined to be gawked and prodded at, and little boys would throw stones at her, seeing if she would flinch whilst the adults would cover their mouths, hoping that the vomit wouldn't spill through their fingers. The little girls who would look up in wonder would be dragged away by the mothers whose faces remained a picture of terror. The whole time, Lana could have been the one to save BlackButterfly from this terrible future. She could have been the one to-

"Earth to Lana! Hello!"

Lana widened her eyes to see Phoebe waving at her.

"Woah, where were you?"

"I'm sorry," Lana replied, "I can't seem to focus at the moment."

"We'll get you another drink," Derek said as he rose from his seat and started towards the bar.

"Seriously though Lanny, I'm getting a little worried about you. I'm starting to regret suggesting this job for you." Phoebe said.

"I'm okay," Lana lied.

"What are you gonna do?"

"I just want to be sure -" Lana paused, "y'know before I start getting the cops involved, I just want to be sure that-"

"What? That there's some weird guy harassing you and an online psychic bitch who's threatening you." Phoebe interjected. "Lana there's a problem here and if you don't report it, I certainly will."

As Phoebe spoke, Lana's eye was caught by something in the distance. At the corner window of Miami's, a figure stood facing her. The windows weren't very large, so she could only see the shoulders and the face of the man that stared right at her. The same man that had tried to get into her apartment a couple of days ago. The same man Bobby had seen on the CCTV cameras. in that moment, all sound around her dissipated as her eyes met with the strangers. He didn't flinch and seemed to relish in her knowing that he was there. She wondered how long he had been watching her. As the activity around her seemed to fade away, Lana saw something else emerge from behind the man. It began to grow larger, towering directly over him. It appeared to be eight or ten feet tall and as it outstretched, its large black wings transformed the second being into what she could only describe as a 'dark angel', Lana felt her breath catch in her throat. She watched in amazement as the two figures looked in at her. This man was the key to BlackButterfly. *He had to be,* she thought.

"I have to go." Lana said abruptly as she stood up and wrapped her jacket around her.

"What? Wait Lana -" Phoebe started

"I'll call you."

"No, Lana stay here," Phoebe stood to grab her arm but Lana had already started for the door. "Derek! Stop her!"

Lana slipped out of the front entrance to Miami's and as Phoebe and Derek burst out on to the street to stop her going any further, they stopped to look at each other with confused expressions lining their faces - she'd completely vanished out of sight.

*

The morning arrived like a hangover.

Painful and unavoidable.

Tyler had drifted in and out of a sleep after he had explored what he could of Tara's home. The events of the day had become amalgamated with events from the past and formed twisted versions of futures that could potentially occur, until these semi-dreams became nothing more than a deep, dark sludge lodged in the back of his mind. He hadn't heard Tara wake yet and his first inclination was to leave the house of secrets and never return. As he lay still with his eyelids clamped shut, he listened to the light drizzle of rain tap at the window and considered how much easier it would be to just return back home and forget this bizarre incident had ever happened. The whole thing had seemed like one of his sludgy dreams anyway, and he was sure he would be able to convince himself that that was all it ever was. He would go home, find a new apartment, find a new job, find a new life and forget it all - except he knew it could never be that easy.

"Would you like some breakfast?"

She appeared right by his bedside. There had been no creaking floorboards, no exhalations or a polite, casual cough to let him know she was there. *How long had she been waiting there? Had he been thinking out loud? Had she heard everything he'd said?*

Tyler flicked his eyes open.

There she was.

She wore a long brown flowing dress and beads of assorted colours were casually draped around her neck. There was a certain light in her eyes that sliced right into him. He realised her presence intimidated him. This woman whom he'd never seen is his life was apparently his sister. The two thoughts still could not gel together in his mind. It was like trying to mix oil and water, no matter how much you stirred them, they would always inevitably end up separating and remaining as individual entities.

"I'll just take a coffee," he grunted, his throat was sore and he wondered if he'd been screaming in the night.

Tara nodded, "I'm afraid I don't have any clean clothes but there's a perfectly good shower in the bathroom next to you, you're welcome to use it."

"Thanks, I packed some things," Tyler replied, there was something a little different about her today. It was as though she had been wiped of any emotion. Her words seemed forced, rehearsed even.

She nodded once more and left the room.

As Tyler tried to formulate his next move, he began to wonder if she had seen him exploring the house last night. Maybe that was what had changed her mood. She knew that he didn't trust her despite her seemingly heartfelt confession. Tyler rolled out of bed and headed to the bathroom. As he stood in the shower, gradually turning the temperature of the water up, he made a pact with himself. He would not leave until he knew exactly what was going on.

She served a breakfast of vegetarian sausages, beans and fried bread and though Tyler tried to concentrate on her and his meal, his gaze would gravitate towards the basement door. Though the eerie music from the night before had since ceased, he could still hear its haunting melody, beckoning him to pull the door open and explore what was down there.

"Is that the basement?" Tyler asked as he finished off the last of his breakfast.

Tara had been stood by the sink, rinsing out a mug, she seemed to jolt slightly at the question.

"Yeah," she replied, "it's out of bounds though, we have a bit of a damp problem around here and it's prone to flooding at this time of the year."

Tyler made a sound of agreement, if this woman really was his sister, he would be able to tell when she was lying and there was something in the way she announced the words that rose suspicion.

"What do you do for work?" Tyler asked.

Once again, she went quiet.

"I work from home," she replied, "catalogues and some phone work."

Tyler nodded.

"What about you?" Tara enquired, seemingly tired of the questions already.

"Well, I'm recently unemployed-" he started.

"Ah, I see," she interrupted.

"What's that supposed to mean?"

"Nothing," Tara began, "well now I know why you've come all this way to see me."

"What? No. I came because you asked me to." Tyler could feel himself getting annoyed and he gripped on to the table to prevent himself from raising his voice.

"I don't know what you mean?"

"You sent me a letter. You asked me to come visit you. That's how I knew your address, I would've called you but I don't have a number for you anymore."

"Tye, I never sent a letter."

Tyler paused.

For a brief moment he wondered if he had conjured up the letter in his mind in a moment of fleeting madness. He wondered if at some point in that day he had suffered a nervous breakdown. Perhaps the hanging housewife had been a figment of his imagination, the letter too.

"I have it in my bag," he rose from the table and bounded up the stairs to retrieve the letter. He recalled how he got a sense that the letter was written by some one else.

"Here," he handed the scrunched up piece of paper to her and he watched her eyes scan over the text.

"I never sent this," she calmly replied.

"Well, it has your address, it's got your name on-"

"That means nothing," she handed the letter back and turned to continue rinsing the dirty kitchen equipment.

"Tara," Tyler said.

She didn't move.

"Tara, look at me."

She placed a glass in the sink and turned to look at him with those eyes that he could not get used to.

"What's going on?" He asked

"Tye, I've told you-"

"You don't look like you, you're behaving strangely, you claim you never sent this letter, I've not heard from you in-in-fuckin' God knows how long and I can't help but feel like there's something weird going on here?" Tyler blurted out.

"I'm not going over this with you again," she answered, her voice remained steady and under control.

"It's like you've been brainwashed or something?"

"Tye, as much as I love you, you're going too far. I think it's time that you left now."

Tyler snorted, there seemed to be no way to get through to her. He stormed out of the kitchen and exited by the front door, slamming it with tremendous force as he bounded down the porch steps.

*

It was that time of the day as the sun would begin to set and the light in New York became a strange in-between of waning daylight and neon illuminations. It would only last for twenty minutes or so but in that short period of time, the world felt slightly more dream-like. If something magical happened, it would most certainly not seem out of place during those few moments. Lana had chased the man over a busy street, carefully dodging two cabs and an elderly gentleman using a stroller. She had quickly turned three corners and sprinted down an entire block but this man, who only seemed to be travelling at a walking pace was gaining more distance on her. Any ideas of danger had vanished from her mind, she was more intent on gaining answers. As he continued in front of her, every now and again, she would spot the large butterfly woman flicker in and out of focus behind him, as though she was a hideous helium balloon and he held the string. She had wanted to call out and have a passer by help her stop him, but she also didn't want to draw any attention to herself. There was the possibility that it could slow her down and she was too focussed on finding out what was going on. Lana found herself in a strange part of the city she had never ventured to before. The streets appeared to be grimier than usual, bags of trash had been left on the sidewalk, windows had been boarded up and plastered with fly posters and graffiti. Small groups of men hung around wearing hoods and sunglasses and they stared at her as she ran past. Some of them cat-called, others made grunts and noises at her.

She ignored them, she just wanted to know why this person was intent on stalking her. She turned a corner and was met with a long alleyway. A large skip stood to one side and fire escape ladders hung overhead. She could see him at the other end. He had turned and was watching her approach him. Lana slowed her pace a little, he was too far away for her to make out any facial features but she could see that his eyes were dark.

"What do you want?" Lana shouted, her voice reverberated off the dirty walls.

He didn't reply, instead he remained fixed in the same position awaiting her next move.

"Why are you following me?" She shouted, realising the irony of the statement as she called out. "I've called the cops already. They're on the way," she lied.

Still, he remained motionless, she could feel his eyes on her body like laser beams. After a few more moments, she began to take a few steps towards him, carefully attempting to judge his next move. He continued to watch as she approached him, Lana realised that one hand was in his pocket and he appeared to be fiddling with something. In the same moment she made the realisation, he began to charge towards her. From out of his pocket, he produced a large knife. The last of the daylight caught the blade and it sparkled in Lana's eyes, her feet felt cemented to the ground and she knew that he would reach her before she could spin around and begin to run in the opposite direction. He tackled her to the floor, forcing her to land on her front and it felt as though he was punching her in the back. Except, the realisation crept in with the third blow, he wasn't punching her.

He was stabbing her.

She counted the number of times the knife slid into her and by the time she reached number five, a cold encompassing darkness took over.

Chapter Thirteen

Rochelle had never experienced an easy day of work. There was always something that upset the balance and she knew that it was the excitement of what the day could bring that had become the main reason she had gotten into the medical profession in the first place. Although she would have to remind herself of that reasoning from time to time. Working in a city hospital provided her with enough junkies and crazies to last a lifetime. Throughout the years she had experienced the urgency of the Accident and Emergency department, the seriousness of the Intensive Care Unit and the complications of the Post-op department and none of it proved to be straight-forward. Somedays she would return home, depleted and unable to feed herself because of the events of the day. Other nurses would tell her to detach and try not to get too involved with her patients but Rochelle was not able to switch that part of her nature on and off like some of the others. She'd tell herself to be strong - that she would do all she could to help other people, that she was a healer, that she wouldn't judge how other people lived their lives, or how they would try to destroy them. Her work was her life and though she tried to lead a separate personal life, it would always seem to take a backseat to her commitments to the hospital. Her nine years of experience had taught her a few things, but the one lesson that took the longest for her to accept was the one of hope. Tragedies occur every day. Toddlers choking, young healthy people with the strictest health regimes diagnosed with terminal diseases, newly married couples in car crashes on their way to the honeymoon destinations. She had seen a lot and though it wasn't good practice to expect the worst, she always did. She couldn't recall what the exact day was when a young woman was rushed in to 'A and E' suffering twelve stab wounds. She'd been discovered unconscious in an alleyway, no personal belongings were found on her so she had been referred in only as Jane Doe. As Rochelle received the details of the attack, she knew that the poor girl would not survive. She'd already lost a lot of blood and there were bound to be multiple severe internal organ wounds as well as severe internal bleeding. Yet she responded as she always did, with willing and good intent. As Jane Doe was rushed in on the stretcher, Rochelle had noted how she looked half dead already. Her features pale, her eyelids gently closed, her arms limp. It was estimated that she had been attacked half an hour or so prior to being found. She knew from experience that this was a substantial chunk of time and it didn't help her chances of survival. The poor girl was rushed into immediate surgery to assess the damage caused and repair what they could. A lot of the time in these situations, they were far from being saved by the time the casualty made it to the surgeon's table. This girl, however, still managed to maintain a consistent pulse and this was a small indication that there was still a potential chance of pulling through. After several hours in surgery, Jane Doe was released back on to a recovery ward, as if by an act of a divine being, most of the stab wounds had missed all the major organs. She'd received a blood transfusion due to the amount that she had lost already and the deep lacerations were carefully stitched up. She was placed on observation and it was noted that if she was able to make it through the night, then her chances of a full recovery would be further increased. To Rochelle's amazement and surprise, Jane Doe pulled through. These sort of miracles didn't happen too often and when they did, Rochelle found herself reassessing her opinions about her work. Sometimes, there was a good outcome. Sometimes, she would be able to tell herself, *it was worth it.*

It had taken two days for Jane Doe to come round after the surgery, she was weak and suffered a tremendous amount of disorientation when she awoke to find herself surrounded by other patients and the distinct aroma of a hospital ward. It had been up to Rochelle to explain to her what had happened and to find out if she had any friends or family that she could contact for her. The girl had told her name was Lana White but had proceeded to murmur several strange things about a black butterfly and a man with inhuman looking eyes. Rochelle had explained that when Lana was feeling a little better, she could contact a member of the police department to take a statement about the attack. There had already been an appeal for witnesses but so far, no one had come forward. This wasn't much of a surprise, when living in a large city most attacks went unnoticed or if witnessed, people are too often afraid to say they saw anything. The truth is that unless the police are able to respond straight away, a lot of the perpetrators got away consequence-free.

Another day passed and Lana's strength had grown considerably. Her health insurance covered the cost of moving to a private room; a perk from her days of escorting. Although she was was still unable to get in touch with any friends due to her cell phone being stolen.

It was a little past six in the evening on a dreary Wednesday when Rochelle managed to find out a little more about how Lana had ended up with twelve stab wounds and left for dead in the gutter.

"Hey Lana, I've brought you your evening feast. We've got mashed potatoes, gravy, peas and I think they call this weird tumour-like grey lump, chicken?" Rochelle joked as she wheeled in the food and placed it on the tray in front of Lana. "How you feelin'?"

"Thanks," Lana replied, shifting herself to a seated position, "a little better, the sleep helps, well-" she paused, "when there's no nightmares."

"Yeah, nightmares don't help," Rochelle placed a knife and fork on either side of the plate and unfolded a napkin, "wanna talk about it?"

Lana appeared slightly preoccupied and after a momentary delay, she shook her head, "it's okay, none of it makes any sense anyway."

"You know, Freud would say otherwise," Rochelle said.

"Freud would say I had deep seated daddy issues and either wanted to sleep with him or murder him."

Rochelle laughed, "I guess you're right, but you know if you wanted to chat about anything, I honestly don't mind lending an impartial ear y'know. No official police statements, just a casual talk."

"Thanks. It's Rochelle isn't it?" Lana enquired.

"Yeah," Rochelle nodded and offered a smile.

"Well thanks Rochelle, it's just all a bit weird and confusing. Being here's been a nice break but I should probably get home soon."

"You're not in danger are you? I mean, the attack - it was just a random thing right?"

Lana went quiet and the blood drained from her face, her eyes began to well up slightly.

"I'm sorry, I don't mean to make things worse for you, I guess I'm just a little concerned for your safety, I mean, if this wasn't a random thing, maybe you should inform the cops right away, they could arrange to have someone watch over you, or at least have you stay with someone you know." Rochelle said, she took a seat next to Lana's bed in attempt to offer some support.

Lana nodded slowly.

"You've not had many visitors, " Rochelle stated, "you do have someone you can stay with for awhile right?"

Lana nodded again.

"I just don't wanna see you back here again," Rochelle offered another sympathetic smile and patted the back of Lana's hand.

"Do you ever feel like you should trust your intuition? Like, you have a gut feeling about something, even if it seems really strange, but you feel like you should just go with it?" Lana said, she had unintentionally lowered her voice as though she was afraid someone was listening in.

Rochelle paused and thought carefully before answering, "I think that if your gut is telling you something then you have to listen to it but only act upon it if it's safe to do so," she paused again and looked Lana right into her eyes, "you're not planning on doing anything stupid are ya?"

An eerie silence descended upon the room and in that moment Rochelle knew that Lana was involved in something far more complicated than she had presumed. From the few conversations that she had had with Lana previously and by the way that she looked, Rochelle was confident that she wasn't involved in drugs or was in trouble with the law in the usual ways she was accustomed to. She'd come across a lot of people who delivered a very convincing act but there was always something in their eyes and their specific choice of words that told her otherwise. Lana seemed like a genuine girl in genuine trouble, and Rochelle knew that the outcome for girls in these sort of situations was rarely a positive one.

Lana hadn't replied to Rochelle's question.

"Can you make me a promise?" Rochelle asked.

Lana didn't answer but met her gaze once more as if to say 'keep talking'.

"If you feel like you're going to make a stupid decision or any decision that you think might have consequences, even if you think they'll be small insignificant consequences, will you promise to tell someone?"

The silence in the room seemed to grow turgid.

"Look, I really shouldn't do this and I don't ever do this, but I'm gonna give you my number and if you ever think that you're going to make a choice that might not be a great choice but your intuition is telling you to do it, maybe run it through me first okay?" Rochelle pulled out her notepad and pen and began to write down her number. "I always have my phone on me so you'll get a reply, but promise me you'll do that?" Rochelle folded up the piece of paper and placed it next to Lana's uneaten food.

Lana was taken aback by Rochelle's gesture but she nodded and returned her warm smile.

*

The rain had eased off slightly yet Tyler would feel the occasional chilly drop land on the nape of his neck, causing him to shiver. The heat of the argument he'd gotten into with Tara a few minutes earlier was beginning to cool off and he scolded himself for getting as wound up as he did. This was certainly a predominant feature of the relationship that he'd had with his sister in the past. There had been countless arguments between them, they would cover a range of topics from the smallest of issues to some of the larger ones. They always ended he same way, one of them would quickly depart only to apologise a few hours later when they've both had time to collect their thoughts. They could never stay mad at each other for long and that was how it had always been. The familiarity of those experiences stung Tyler as he began to walk down Cemetery Road. He still had difficulty in accepting that this woman was in no doubt behaving just like his sister would, and despite the obvious physical differences, there was just something else that was not quite right about the whole situation. Tyler placed his hands in his pockets as he walked. The breeze was biting and he scolded himself for not thinking to grab a jacket as he left the house but he told himself it might awaken a part of the truth that he had not since accessed. Since Tara's house was one of the last on the road, he retraced his steps back from the way he had arrived the day previously. He observed that just like before, the houses looked lived in, though it appeared there was no sign of life within them. There were no lights glowing from the inside, no cats scratching at the front doors ready to greet their owners and have breakfast served to them. The stillness of the street made Tyler feel incredibly uneasy and he was reminded of the thought of these house being nothing more than 'show homes.' A fake pretence in order to pick up a sale.

This is the life you could have.

This could be yours.

Tyler shuddered at the thought, he considered that he would feel more at home in a funeral parlour than he would in any of these seemingly empty vessels. As he continued down the street, he felt compelled to investigate Tara's neighbours, perhaps they could offer a clue as to why she had changed so dramatically or maybe confirm that he had indeed crossed over into the town of Stepford.

Tyler slowed his pace and tried his best to look as inconspicuous as possible. Though the houses looked dead inside, he couldn't shake the distinct feeling that he was being watched. He realised that that sort of feeling would not be so out of place considering that within such a small street, everyone was bound to know everyone else, so a strange man coyly perusing the neighbourhood was likely to garner some attention. He passed the house next to Tara's, a similar sized building obviously built at the same time as all the others. However, some of its features were subtly different. He observed less lower floor windows and more upper floor windows, the porch area was considerably smaller and the front garden was surrounded by a small wooden fence. Tyler tried his best to see if he could see any movement inside but could only make out the gloomy silhouettes of what appeared to be antiquated furniture. He continued down the road, casually glancing up at the houses as he passed them in the hope that there was confirmation of any life in this area and that Cemetery Road wasn't in fact an ironic name. It was as he was passing the third house down that he noticed something a little unusual. Tyler stopped and dropped down to one knee, pretending that he was tying his shoelace so he could gather a little more time to look at the house without looking too suspicious. Above the front door, etched into the wood was a large symbol. It stuck out considerably since all the houses were immaculate but this crudely carved shape ruined the image of what would otherwise be a house kept in perfect condition. Tyler did not recognise the symbol, it consisted of three different sized triangles which all interlocked together. It looked like something a primary school child had done, the lines were crooked and appeared deeper in parts but there was something odd about how it looked. It seemed purposeful as though the occupants had intentionally left it there but it was completely out of place with the rest of the perfect characterisation of the road. Tyler carefully slipped his phone out of his pocket and snapped a picture of the symbol, he was determined to find out if it had any sort of significance. Tyler put his phone away and carried on down the road.

The layout of the houses was unconventional, he had never seen a street where the distance between each building was considerably sparse. It also looked highly unusual that there were more residences on one side of the road than the other. He tried to conclude that this was how it was in the part of the country although he'd visited enough small villages in the past to know that the uneven house placement on Cemetery Road was downright bizarre. Tyler continued farther down towards the graveyard and passed another house with the same strange symbols etched in the woodwork above the front entrance. It too, was crudely scratched into the surface but it was unmistakably the same pattern that had been carved above the door of the other house. Tyler was reminded of runic symbols but he had never seen one that looked quite like these ones. Runes tended to be of a much more simple design, yet these had slightly more detail than he would expect. Tyler quickened his pace, he was curious to see if any more houses had the same symbols depicted above their entrances. As he approached the end of the road, he noted another house with the exact same symbols on the front, he once again quickly snapped a picture on his phone and began to turn back to Tara's house. There was something unsettling about observing these three houses with same strange symbols presented at their entrances.

"Everything okay there?"

Tyler turned to see an older man stood a few feet away from him. He quickly dropped his phone in his pocket, knowing that the man had seen him take a picture.

"Yeah, yeah, fine thanks. Just taking a little morning stroll," Tyler replied.

"I see," the man looked him up and down, obviously curious as to why he was there. Tyler answered his question before he could ask it.

"I'm just visiting my sister, Tara Hamilton. You know her?" Tyler asked.

The old man squinted and didn't reply straight away. Tyler noted his clothes looked old and worn and there were numerous stains and patches of fabric that had faded with age. He wore a cap that looked as though it had once adorned a tartan print design, but it too had faded and looked ready to be thrown out.

"I do, she's been a neighbour of mine for a good many year now," he smiled bearing a set of crooked teeth, "quiet lass, keeps herself to herself," the old man appeared to chuckle to himself but Tyler failed to see the joke.

"Well, it was nice meeting you," Tyler said as he started to walk back.

"Will you be staying long?" The old man enquired, the strange smirk still stretched across his face.

"I shouldn't expect so."

"We'll see," the old man murmured under his breath.

Tyler turned to face the man, "excuse me?"

"Enjoy your stay," he smiled.

"Right," Tyler replied, knowing that the old man was acting coy, "I will."

The old man continued to stay put as Tyler walked away, and although he didn't turn around, he could feel his eyes on him the entire stretch back. Tyler couldn't be sure if he was relieved to find out that Tara's neighbours existed or that they seemed to be altogether quite unlike anyone he'd ever encountered before.

Chapter Fourteen

Once visiting hours were over and the last of the friends and family are ushered out of the building, a strange stillness descended upon the recovery wards. Quite unlike the opposite end of the hospital where countless ambulances efficiently dropped off casualties like deliveries on a conveyor belt and then proceeded to head back out to the streets. The doctors and staff took their turns to work tirelessly ensuring that everyone was getting enough care. The recovery ward however, was an entirely different experience. There was the steady beeping of electronic devices, the faint suck and hush of respirators in rooms a little bit farther down the corridor. Sometimes the soft shuffle of footfall on linoleum would occasionally perforate the hypnotic effect of the rhythmic equipment as nurses completed their checks on each ward. From time to time, the sound of muffled conversation and music from the television room at the very far end of the ward drifted through the walls. Lana found some comfort in these sounds. Unlike living on her own at home, the repetition of familiar sound was soothing. She didn't feel too alone.

For Lana, waking up in a hospital bed, groggy from the immensely strong painkillers that had numbed her nervous system and confused as to how she had ended up there, the recollection of the events leading up to that fateful encounter had plagued her. As each of the memories returned to her, she wished that amnesia had taken them all. Unfortunately, the recollections were vivid and unsparing. Her morphine-infused dreams relayed stories of BlackButterfly, immortalised as a ten foot moth-girl with no face hunting her down through a labyrinth of various other horrors. Sometimes the monster that had stalked her previously would make an appearance, yet instead of stabbing her with a large stainless steel knife, he would commit his crime with a rusty spear. It would penetrate her body completely and the sensation of it ripping through her flesh and through her spine was searingly painful. It burnt like a hot poker creating a grotesque sizzling sound as it tore through her internal organs. During these delusions she would always be running away from something. Always the mouse, never the cat.

Her waking hours, despite the pangs of pain if she moved a little too much or coughed slightly aggressively were however, less terrifying. The staff had been nothing but friendly and supportive and did all they could to make her feel as comfortable as possible. She had quickly bonded with Rochelle and noted her advice whenever she would offer it. She reminded her of Phoebe and she would feel guilty for leaving her and Derek the way she did. She desperately wanted to contact them to let them know she was safe and well but had no way of getting in touch. She could only assume that her phone had been stolen either by the stalker or by the person who found her and though it angered her that someone would do such a thing, she wasn't surprised. She would try and concentrate on reaffirming how grateful she was that they had called for an ambulance. The outcome could have been entirely different otherwise.

As she lay there, drifting in and out of sleep, she tried not to wonder what had happened to BlackButterfly yet her plea for help still seemed fresh in her mind. She'd open up another layer of guilt and would absorb it, it seemed to sting each of her still-fresh stab wounds like painful reminders. One afternoon. Lana had cautiously peeled back some of the damp dressing that covered her abdomen. She discovered that the injuries were still fresh and fluctuated in colour, parts were angry red and raw, other areas blossomed in various shades of green and black. The criss-cross stitches that tied the flesh together had reminded her of spider legs. She tried to accept the guilt of letting BlackButterfly down but it caused her to become restless, her feet kicked tirelessly and all her muscles ached.

Lana flicked her eyelids open, she had heard footsteps at the far end of the corridor. She stayed motionless and held her breath so she could hear the steps better. There was something distinctly familiar about the heaviness of the steps and the urgency of the pace. Lana had come to realise that most of the nurses tended to wear trainers or light shoes since they were on their feet for a large part of the day. She had never known any of them to wear any footwear that would make such a distinctive clomping sound. The realisation hit her like she had been slammed in the face with a hot iron. She knew exactly who those particular footsteps belonged to and this time she wasn't coming for him, he was coming for her.

She immediately reached up and pulled the red emergency cord to alert the nurse station that she was in trouble. She observed a small red light began to flash above her bed. Lana bolted upright, though the sharp movement caused the stitches to pull at her skin causing a dull ache to begin. She held her stomach where the pain throbbed and dropped her legs to the floor. The hospital had provided slippers which she efficiently pushed her feet into. *Now what?* She wondered, there were two options - run or hide, and with the extent of her injuries, Lana wasn't sure she could run far without tearing the wounds open again. The footsteps were getting increasingly closer, she knew it was only a matter of seconds before he would enter the room and finish the job. *How did he find me? How did he know I was still alive?* The questions began to build but she knew she couldn't entertain the answers at that moment. Time was precious. Lana looked under the bed but realised it would be too obvious of a hiding place, she toyed with the option of going out into the corridor and attempting to outrun her assailant but she knew it would be far too risky. The only other option would be to hide within the small ensuite bathroom attached adjacent to the room. She quickly staggered over to the room and just as she pulled the door open and slipped inside, she heard someone enter the main room. She pressed her back against the door and prayed that it was a nurse that had come to her rescue. She squeezed her eyes tight, *please God, please God, please God*, she silently chanted. There was silence on the other side of the door, *maybe he left? Maybe he thought he got the wrong room? Maybe he got caught?* Just as she was contemplating what had happened, she heard something come from the other-side of the door. It sounded like a soft growl. She turned slightly to get a better listen, though afraid to press her ear right up against the door. She'd seen far too many horror films where the inquisitive victim had received a precisely placed knife through the door and into the head, and she had already had her fill of stab wounds for the time being.

"I know you're in there."

His voice sounded like thorns on sandpaper. Deep and coarse.

Lana held her hand over her mouth to prevent her whimpers from escaping. She felt a little pressure push against the door and she wondered if he was preparing to smash the door down.

"Come out, come out, wherever you are," he said.

It sounded as though his mouth was pressed right up against the crack in the door. He sounded intimately close and it caused her heart to palpitate.

Lana didn't respond but witnessed the handle begin to move just as it had done back at her apartment. She gripped it tightly, preventing it from being moving any further. The bathroom had been fitted with a very basic lock, designed to give easy entry in case there were any medical emergencies. Lana knew she'd have to rely on her weight against the door and control of the handle to keep the stalker out. She'd have to wait it out until a staff member turned up to assist. *Where were they?* She wondered. The pressure on the door began to increase as though he was testing her strength and enjoying the tease. She felt it began to shake, as though he was beginning to use his own body weight to force the door open. Each impact grew more intense and Lana tried her best to keep her body steady but she was forced forwards and backwards with each thud and she was beginning to lose her grip on the handle. Lana continued to try and keep her body taunt and firm against the door and caught a glimpse of herself in the mirror. There was only a dim light in the room, but she witnessed the fear in her eyes, it glowed like a night-light but she also saw something else. It looked to be a large shadow directly projected on the door behind her. It had a semi-human shape, but instead of arms, there were wings and they began to outstretch, they extended out of her view in the mirror and Lana fought back the tears that were beginning to appear in the corners of her eyes. *No,* she thought, *I'm sorry.* The door was beginning to come away from the hinges and Lana was finding it increasingly difficult to keep her body propped against the weakening doorway. She felt something warm around her abdomen area and looked down to see her belly bleeding. The sheer force of the numerous impacts had ripped out some of the stitches and one of the stab wounds had re-opened. She used her free hand to put pressure on the gash. The blood felt hot and sticky but she continued to press down as hard as possible. In the next moment, she was thrown across the room as the door was smashed open. Lana slowly turned around and saw him standing over, the hideous green glow flashed in his eyes and a sinister smile appeared on his face.

*

Tyler had waited outside Tara's house for a few minutes in an attempt to gather his thoughts and try and make sense of the situation that was becoming increasingly stranger and stranger by the moment. Very little of what he'd picked up on was making sense at this point and he couldn't be sure if he was losing his mind or whether everyone else was losing theirs. As he began to make his way inside again, still unsure of how to play it with his sister, his phone began to ring. It was someone he had not expected to hear from again.

"Hi Geoff?" Tyler answered with trepidation.

"Hi, I hope it's not a bad time to call you?" He asked, he sounded particularly awake compared to Tyler's morning growl.

"No, not at all," Tyler replied, "how was the rest of your trip?"

"If I'm being honest, less fun after you left."

Tyler could feel himself blushing, "likewise," he answered.

"I just thought I'd check in and wish you a good morning. I know most guys would usually text or whatever but I guess I'm old fashioned," Geoff said.

Tyler tried to think of a witty comeback but came back dry, "that's not a bad thing."

"So how's the family?"

Tyler found himself unable to answer the question straight away.

"You still there Tyler?"

"Yeah, yeah, sorry," he replied, "it's been a strange twenty four hours."

"Let me guess, like an episode of The Twilight Zone?" Geoff joked.

Tyler laughed, "you have no idea how incredibly accurate that statement is."

"It's the same with me, I swear every time I visit my family, I could swear I'm taking part on some hidden camera show," Geoff paused. "You're good though right? You don't sound like yourself?"

"I wish I could answer that question honestly right now but we barely know each other-"

"Well, what better way to get to know someone than by burdening them with some deep rooted family drama. I'm all ears," Geoff said.

"Thanks, listen, how about we talk later on?" Tyler answered, he could feel prying eyes upon him.

"Sure thing," Geoff replied, "I hope it all works out okay for you. My advice though, is keep the peace. It makes things much easier in the long run."

"Thanks Geoff, I will remember that. Speak later." Tyler disconnected the call and turned around to see Tara standing at the dining room window, her eyes were fixed directly on him. Her face looked washed out and grey, and there was something distinctly inhuman about the way she stood perfectly motionless. Tyler resisted the urge to wave at her to make her aware that that her presence had been noticed but before he could contemplate any further action she turned away from the window and her silhouette faded into the heavy darkness of the room. Tyler knew very well that she been stood there to be noticed.

"Who were you talking to?"

Tyler had entered the house to find Tara standing at the end of the corridor, her arms crossed over her chest and fire in her eyes.

"A friend of mine," he replied, holding back on becoming defensive with her. He knew that if he wanted to uncover what was going on, he was going to need to keep the peace just as Geoff had advised him.

"A friend?"

"Yes, he was just checking in with me, made sure I arrived safely," Tyler said.

"You were talking about me," she stated firmly.

Tyler didn't know how to respond to her statement. She wasn't too far from the truth but he hadn't mentioned any of the strange occurrences he had encountered, although he had desperately longed for reassurance that he wasn't losing his mind. "Your name was never mentioned," he eventually answered.

"Well, I need you gone today, I have guests coming around tonight," Tara said, her arms stayed firmly in position in an act of defiance.

"You need me gone? So much for the warm welcome then," Tyler wished he could bite his tongue but the words spilled out.

"I never asked you to come," she said as she shifted uncomfortably and lowered her voice, "look Tye, it's been really great seeing you, it has. I just wish it could be-" she paused and looked away from him, "different."

"What do you mean Tara?"

"Please Tye, listen to me, just leave. Today." The fire in her eyes began to return.

"Okay, okay, I give in, I'll leave but you'll have to give me a little more time, I'll need to get a cab back to the station. Can I not just stay one more night?" Tyler said, he did his best impression of a defenceless animal.

"I'm hosting a dinner party tonight, you can't stay," she answered firmly.

"Alright, I get it, I'm not invited to your party. I'll stay out of the way, I'll pretend as if I'm not here. I'll stay in the bedroom with the door closed reading my book. Just so I can stay the night. Please sis." Tyler asked.

"I don't know," she appeared to be weighing up his option.

"Look, even if I need the bathroom, I'll pee in a bottle or something. No one will have any idea that I'm there."

She looked at him closely, "okay, one more night," she gave in, "but you have to stay in your room. My guests won't be expecting any extra visitors. You understand?" Tara instructed.

"I do. I understand completely," Tyler nodded to emphasise his point, "thank you."

Tara reciprocated his nod and he couldn't be sure but he thought he saw a small smile flash on her face momentarily.

"Can I help you prepare?" Tyler asked.

"Actually, yes you can."

The atmosphere had changed. Even the air that surrounded Tyler felt different, he breathed it in as though renewed and ready for whatever challenges were yet to come. This was an unusual sensation for him, he'd often spent his days fighting off any potential challenges. He'd grown accustomed to being able to find the perfect excuse not to attend the Christmas party at work or skilfully avoiding any sort of social situation that might cause his anxiety to spike, sending him into a dithering mess. He had refined these skills well enough so that not a single person had suspected otherwise. Most of the time he was fine - unexpected situations would rear their ugly faces and instinctively, he dealt with whatever it was. For most people, their confidence grows with age, but it had been quite the opposite for Tyler although he did his best to keep his head above water for the majority of the time. This change in atmosphere had been prefixed by the seemingly smooth transition of a personality change of Tara. Though he still had a sense that she was his sister despite the exterior of a strange older woman, it seemed as though the less-serious Tara had made an appearance and was excited about the prospect of Tyler helping her prepare for the dinner party. His agreement to stay out of sight that night had given her a new lease of life and she had solidified this by skipping into the kitchen whilst humming a generic tune and becoming largely more animated. Tyler could see flashes of the old Tara right there in that older woman's body, it was in the way she hummed and the uneven bounce in her step. It was uncanny and as much as Tyler wanted to probe further, he thought it would be best to play along and see what information he could uncover without rousing any suspicion. Tara had mentioned that she was going upstairs to clean up and get changed. A few moments after she left, Tyler quietly approached the basement door and tried the handle.

It was still locked.

He casually looked around the kitchen to see if the key was anywhere to be found but he had no luck. He knew that there was something down there that she didn't want him to see and he was determined to find out what it was. Something told him that whatever was residing in the underbelly of this seemingly perfect house was the key to eventually unlocking this surreal secret. He searched in as many obvious places as possible only to no avail, he concluded that she must keep the key on her at all times and this further added to his anxiety about the whole situation. Tyler, guided by a thirst, approached the refrigerator and pulled it open to pour himself a glass of orange juice when he noticed something jutting out slightly on the top of the unit. It was a small dark shape. He reached up and grabbed a hold of the curious object. As soon as his fingers made contact with the cold metal - the shape seemed all too familiar, in that moment, he realised he had struck gold. He had found what he was looking for - the key to the basement. Excitement and nerves washed over him, his first instinct was to quickly unlock the door and reveal what Tara was keeping so secretive down there. However, he also knew that he didn't have much time to investigate so he fought back the urge to open the door and begin snooping around. He immediately felt better now that he knew how to get access to the room. *Tonight,* he thought, *I will find out what's down there.*

Chapter Fifteen

That moment, with their eyes firmly locked into each others seemed to last an entire lifetime. Lana knew that she had no advantage over him whilst lay on the floor with her wound now freshly opened and stinging in a succession of painful throbs. He took a step towards her, his grin growing more menacing.

"What are you waiting for? Just finish me off then!" Lana shouted, she was attempting to create as much noise as possible whilst still keeping her attacker none the wiser that she was trying to draw attention to the situation. He took another step towards her and Lana saw movement in the room behind him. It was Rochelle, she had come to her rescue after she had pulled the alert cord earlier on.

"Why do you wanna hurt me? Can't you just leave me alone?" Lana wailed, making it crystal clear to Rochelle that her guest had not been invited. "Why?" She screamed.

Lana watched Rochelle slip out of view, she returned a few seconds later gripping the empty tray of which she'd brought Lana's dinner on earlier. Lana slowly adjusted herself so that she was in a better position to get up and dash past the intruder when the timing was right. It wasn't going to be easy, especially with the sensation of fresh hot blood oozing out of her. There was an unspoken communication between Rochelle and Lana in those few moments. Lana's clarification that her attacker was intent on doing more harm was all that was needed and Rochelle smashed the tray over his head with all of her strength. It vibrated and clanged and if Lana was not nursing her open wound while lay on the floor in a petrified state, the sound of the tray hitting the stalker and the way his eyes rolled backwards would have seemed slightly more comical. Though when he turned to see who it was that had attacked him, the look of horror on Rochelle's face would have quickly dispelled any sense of humour. She instantly retaliated by using the tray to smash against his face once more and as Lana was rising to her feet, she saw the side of his jaw become dislocated and hung loosely to the side of his face. He grabbed on to it as though it was about to fall to the floor and lunged at Rochelle. She side stepped him and screamed to Lana to escape out of the room as quickly as she could. Lana had gotten to her feet and started to limp out of the door. She realised she must have also pulled a muscle when he smashed the door down. The attacker was reaching for Rochelle who had backed into the furthest corner of the room, she consistently hit him in the face with the tray and from where Lana was stood, it looked like Rochelle was batting the features clearly off his skull. He kept his hands placed firmly on his face, trying to protect himself from any more blows. Rochelle signalled with her eyes for Lana to get out but she knew she could not leave her whilst attempting to defend herself against this monster. Lana hobbled through the door, her hand still pressed against the wound on her abdomen and turned back to her attacker who was just about to raise his fist to Rochelle.

"Hey!" Lana yelled, "hey, you fucker! You want me? Come and get me!"

She immediately turned back out of the room and started to run down the corridor as fast as possible. She prayed that her plan had worked, she knew there would be no turning back at this point. As Lana managed to get ten steps away from the room, she heard his heavy footsteps echo down the corridor.

He had begun to chase her.

"Help! Somebody help us!" Lana screamed with all her might but her voice was growing weak along with her body. She was not sure she could even make it to the end of the corridor which in that moment, seemed to stretch on endlessly. The next ward was through a pair of double doors at the end and she knew that if she could make it through them, then someone would have to be able to hear her.

"Help! Please!" Her throat was burning and another panic about losing her voice set in. *What if I make it to the doors and then I'm unable to call for help?* She tried hard not to let the thoughts in but within half a second, she had already allowed a handful of dreadful 'what ifs' in without their approval. His footsteps were growing louder, she knew it would only be a few moments when his dry, calloused hand would reach out and grab her by the hair, tugging her backwards and into his arms. She knew there would be very little chance of any survival if it got to that point.

"Help! Anyone!" She gave it one last try in the hope that someone would come through the doors any moment and save her. The footsteps were right behind her now and the door was still several yards away. Lana expelled all the air from her body and pushed with all her might to get a final sprint out of her aching legs.

If she could just get to the door-

Lana had fallen over her feet and the next few seconds seemed to play out in extreme slow motion. The beige and mahogany crisscrossed square patterns on the vinyl flooring began to approach her face. Her hands started to reach out in front of her, hoping to lessen the force of the impact. The footsteps were directly behind her now and a long dark shadow loomed over her. *This is it,* she thought, *all over now.* Lana hit the floor, only one hand managed to make contact with the surface, she watched as her frail wrist bent out of shape and waited to hear it snap. *What would a broken wrist be now if she was merely seconds away from death?* Her wrist was somehow saved and she rolled on to her side, fully aware that her stab wound had now been completely ripped open again and her nightshirt was covered in blood. She landed on her hip and the momentum forced her to roll on her back, at first she closed her eyes. She didn't want to give her attacker the satisfaction of seeing her scared. *Not this time,* she thought, *this time he won't get to see.* She clamped her eyelids shut and sealed her lips. She wasn't going to scream either. She could feel his presence over her and Lana waited to feel a cold blade slip into chest.

Except she felt nothing.

She wondered if she had now in fact died. If she had surpassed any sensation of physical pain. Mortality had been whisked away from her in an instant and she was now about to embark on a new level of transcendental bliss. Lana wasn't religious, she expected death to be nothing more than an eternal slumber. That sensation of not remembering the moment you slipped into sleep, only to be recalled groggily the next morning. Except with death, there never would be a 'next morning'. Yet she could still feel the cold floor jutting into her shoulder blades and the unmistakeable smell of the hospital still lingered.

"Lana, get up."

The voice was not that of her attackers, it sounded like a heavenly creature and though Lana was still handling the possibility that she was in fact still alive, the idea of an angelic guardian safely guiding her to a large set of exuberant white gates seemed plausible. Though this was the voice of a different type of angel. A healer by the name of Rochelle.

"Lana, he's gone, get up."

Lana felt someone tug at her arm and begin to pull her upwards.

"We need to get you cleaned up."

"Wh-what do you mean, he's gone?" Lana whispered, her voice was on the verge of completely disappearing.

"When you ran out of the room, he left in the opposite direction. I guess, he knew he would be caught otherwise," Rochelle said.

Lana opened her eyes, the bright overhead lights stung her pupils but she could just about make out a dark fuzzy shape hovering over her. As her eyes adjusted, Rochelle's face came in to view. She smiled and Lana wondered how she managed to keep so calm and relaxed given that she may have also been murdered in cold blood a few moments earlier. As though predicting her thought, Rochelle replied, "you'd be surprised how many similar incidents I've had to deal with like that in the past."

Lana tried to say thank you but the shock of what had happened was beginning to set in. She wanted to tell Rochelle how much she was grateful for not allowing that bastard to take her life but she also wanted to tell her to leave her be, she didn't want to drag another innocent person into her homicidal mess. There had to be a strong reason why she was wanted dead and Lana could't understand what it was that had gotten her into this much trouble but she would be damned if she was to get anyone else involved.

"You have to let me leave," Lana whispered.

Rochelle appeared to be taken aback by the question, "what are you talking about?"

"I'm obviously not safe here, which means neither is anyone else around me, including you."

"Not here, not now. You're bleeding out Lana, let me ring through to reception to hold off anyone else coming and we'll discuss what needs to happen while I get you stitched back up again." Rochelle placed a hand on Lana's shoulder in a gesture of alliance.

Chapter Sixteen

Cemetery Road stretched on farther than Tyler had first assumed. The way it twisted and meandered gave the impression that it was nothing more than a country lane housing a local church and a few mismatched houses. Yet as Tara carefully drove from her house to the local town centre, the road soon opened up into a huge expanse of luscious green fields and disused wastelands. The fringe of the horizon presented endless forests where most of the trees had lost their leaves and their skeletal branches reminded Tyler of bony hands bursting from graves, clawing at the sky for one last attempt at life. Tara drove with extreme caution, her eyes remained fixed to the road and her knuckles grew white from gripping the steering wheel with such strength. She had returned from upstairs dressed in another long flowing dress, this one was mahogany coloured and matched the woodwork of her home. The garment had added another ten years to her appearance and Tyler wondered whether this was an intentional action. He was still struggling to accept the mystifying situation yet when she spoke, he knew undeniably, that it was Tara that was behind the words. He'd occasionally glance over at her behind the wheel, attempting to catch a glimpse of the truth. It had taken over thirty minutes to escape the acres and acres of fresh pasture and most of their journey had been occupied with silence. Tyler had been carefully concocting a plan of visiting the basement that evening and Tara seemed preoccupied with something. Her breezy demeanour from earlier on had since been replaced with one of deep gravity. Tyler had attempted a few moments of small talk as they prepared for the journey but was met either with a one word answer or no acknowledgement of his question at all. It was clearly evident that something was on her mind. It had just turned one p.m. when they arrived in the small town, which consisted of a square-shaped piece of land occupied by a few small businesses; a number of restaurants, a gift shop and a convenience store. Central to the square was a small garden area with a focal point of a large statue that appeared to be perhaps a member of royalty or an unknown saint. As they parked up, Tyler had pointed to the statue and asked if Tara knew who the statue was of, she replied that it was the founder of Edenville and he noticed her mood had changed once again - she was becoming slightly more animated. They walked from the car to the large convenience store, grabbing a trolley on the way and entered the building.

"What time are your guests arriving?" Tyler asked.

Tara threw a bag of potatoes in the trolley and glanced at her watch, "about six," she said, "we should have enough time."

"To prepare?"

"Yes."

They walked around the store collecting bits and pieces for the evening, a few of the locals turned to look at Tyler, it was almost as though he'd be unwillingly assigned a blinking neon light that flashed with the word 'outsider' to all that passed by. He tried his best to ignore the people glancing at him from the side of their eyes. Their hushed whispers would come to a halt whenever they passed them.

"Why do I feel like everyone is staring at me?" Tyler whispered to Tara as he glanced back down the aisle to see two women looking directly at him.

"It's a small town. If you haven't shopped here before, you'll be noticed. Everyone knows everyone here," Tara replied as she continued to push the trolley, eyeballing the shelves and shelves of products, "damn, I forgot to get wine, we'll have to go back."

Tyler found her comment strange, "but nobody seems to say hello to you, normally there's some acknowledgement between people that recognise each other."

Tara replied almost immediately, "Edenville is not like that. Every town is different, you can't expect everywhere to be the same."

There was a coldness in the way she spoke the words and Tyler had to hold himself back from getting into a full blown debate with her. There was one thing he could agree with her on - and that was that Edenville certainly was unlike any other place he had visited. In an attempt to change the topic and to stop overanalysing the less-than-obvious stares and the stifled whispers, he made a suggestion to Tara. "How about we go to that Italian place across the street and get some dinner before we head back."

"We won't have time," Tara replied, "we need to get back as soon as possible."

"We'll be thirty minutes tops, my treat," Tyler offered whilst trying to banish the image of his waning bank balance in his mind.

After a few moments of silence and what appeared to be a considerable amount of internal debate, she nodded in agreement.

The restaurant was larger on the inside than what it had appeared from the solitary window at the entrance. The aroma of fresh bread caused Tyler's stomach to begin to rumble and he realised it had been a long time since he had sat down to a proper meal. His stay at Tara's had been maintained on a simple diet of snacks and leftovers, she had not been prepared for his visit and her food stock was minimal at least. The invitation to dinner was an opportunity for Tyler to get Tara away from her usual surroundings. He hoped that this change may make her feel more open and less resilient in revealing the truth of her situation. The fact that she was able to willingly leave her residence had laid to rest his theory that this woman who claimed to be his sister was being held hostage. *Perhaps she was keeping the real Tara locked away somewhere?* His brain was continually assessing the situation and trying to dissemble and pick apart the truth from the clues in front of him. There was no denying there was more that was going on beneath the surface, he just needed to create a crack first before he could begin to extract the truth.

The host directed them to a seat next to the window and they each ordered cokes whilst they perused the menu. Tara was displaying a few anxious behaviours and Tyler wondered what the real reason behind her quick glances at her watch and out of the window was. He wanted to make her feel as comfortable as possible in the hope that he might be able to unlock the truth of what really was going on.

"Do you ever hear from anyone back home?" Tyler dove in at the deep end, relinquishing the quiet opportunity and the chance that she wouldn't have too much time to skirt around the question.

"No," she replied, her eyes unmoving from the menu, her grip so tight that the menu appeared to shake slightly.

"Me neither, been a while since I've heard from anyone. Although I hear Pete's married and settled down now. Two kids. Who would've thought?" Tyler contributed.

"Good for him," Tara said.

Tyler glanced around the restaurant, for a local eatery at that time of day, he was surprised to see that about two thirds of the tables were occupied. The diners seemed too preoccupied with their food and drinks to treat him the same way they did in the convenience store. A dull wave of chatter and clinking washed over the restaurant while soft instrumental music played over the ambient sounds. Tyler was pleasantly surprised with the restaurant, the empty glasses at the table gleamed like expensive crystal and the napkins were folded within an inch of perfection. The menus had been carefully designed with the restaurant name 'Dom's' printed clearly on the front in cursive writing. There was a certain charm that exuded the restaurant and under different circumstances, Tyler would have taken the opportunity to relish in the pleasant experience. He was however, far too determined in uncovering the truth about what was happening with Tara to enjoy the surrounding comforts. She hadn't been very forthcoming with conversation so Tyler tried again.

"Do you host these dinner parties often?" He asked, placing the menu down to signify he'd made his decision.

"We take turns," she answered firmly.

"That's nice, it's good to know you've made some new friends around here."

"I want to be sure that you'll be staying out of the way tonight. I can't risk you ruining this evening."

The statement appeared to be served with the slight pretence of a threat and Tyler took a moment to formulate his reply.

"Well yes, I said I would. I don't want to ruin your plans," he paused, "but Tara-"

Her eyes suddenly met his over the top of her menu.

"Do you not want to introduce me to them? I mean, I'm family, I'm your brother. It might be nice to meet your friends?" Tyler spoke softly as not to provoke another prickly response.

"Not tonight," she said, her eyes flicked back to the text on the menu.

"Can I ask why?"

"I said, not tonight Tye."

"But-"

"Do you need me to fucking spell this out for you?"

The tone suddenly changed once again, and although she didn't scream the words, she spoke them with such ease and control that it chilled Tyler to the core. They had experienced their fair share of arguments and disagreements in the past but the way she responded seemed like it had come from an entirely different person. Her retaliation rendered him speechless for a few moments and before he could offer any form of reply, they were interrupted by the waiter who proficiently took down their orders. Tara had requested a green leaf salad and lasagne with the skill of a professional actress capable of switching her mood depending on the scene. She accentuated the end of her order with a beaming smile and her eyes glowed pleasantly. Tyler had to clear his throat before he could relay his order back to the waiter. The entire time, he could feel Tara's eyes bearing right through him as though they were to attempting to extract something from him. He couldn't help but feel like the tables had been turned and she was trying to reveal something about him in that very moment. It took a couple of attempts to make his order without stuttering over the occasional syllable. Once the waiter had departed, Tyler looked over to Tara and with as much ease and control as he could muster, he finally replied to her previous question.

"I don't know what's going on here and you're making it pretty obvious that you don't want me to know but I swear to God, if you've done something to my sister or you know what has happened to her, I will rip you apart without a second thought."

Tara remained motionless and after a few heavy seconds, he watched the corners of her mouth raise to form a smile.

"What's so funny?" Tyler enquired, he could feel the temperature of his blood raise a few degrees.

She continued to smile, "you were always so protective of me little brother. It should have been the other way around."

Tyler was once again, taken aback by her surprising response, he leaned in closer to her.

"What's going on?" He whispered.

She leaned in slightly too, "Tye, you have absolutely nothing to worry about. You should never have come, in fact I should never have let you through my front door but I did. After tonight, you have to go and forget about this whole episode and please, forget about me."

"What are you talking about? I just can't forget you ever exist? You're the only family have left?"

"Please." She said.

"You've not asked anything about my life or why it was that I came here? You know, just a few days ago I was planning on-" Tyler stopped himself, "I was in a bad place and then your letter came and I thought to myself that it was a sign. I thought that this was a way of my sister saying that she was looking out for me, that she wanted to protect me from all the shitty things that were going on-" he took a breath and fought back the creeping tears, "yet here I am, sat in a restaurant in this fuckin' creepy graveyard of a town with a woman who looks nothing like my sister who is telling me to leave and forget she ever exists? Do you know how crazy this all sounds? I swear I feel like I am losing my fuckin' mind!"

Tyler wasn't aware that he had increased the volume of his voice and that a few of their fellow diners had turned to look in their direction to find out what the raucous was about. Tara continued to look at him, her face was emotionless, nothing he had said had any form of impact on her and he felt like slamming his fists down on the table, smashing the perfect looking crockery and screaming at the top of his lungs. He lowered his voice and leaned in to her, "I should just call the police, let them sort this mess out."

As soon as he finished speaking, a loud scream erupted from the other side of the restaurant and Tyler turned to see where the sound had come from. The remaining chatter and general din evaporated in that moment and the other diners turned to see who was in distress. In the very corner of the room, a woman rose her table and screamed again. From where he was sat, Tyler struggled to fully see what was happening. The woman was sickly thin, she was dressed in evening wear - a pencil thin dress that clung to her less than shapely frame. Her thin, bone-white arms began to stretch out towards Tyler, her eyes firmly fixed in his direction. He realised she was pointing directly at him, her wide glassy eyes were pinned open in a look of absolute terror. The man that she was sat with looked on at her in disbelief, it was clear that her response had come from out of the blue. The woman had turned deathly pale and her thin shoulder length hair clung to her perspiring face. She screamed again and with her finger still pointed, she began to stagger from her side of the restaurant to where Tyler sat. There was no way he could move from his seat, the entire situation had caused him to freeze to the spot, his heart raced with a quick succession of hammer-like thumps and dread descended over the entirety of his body. *Why is this woman screaming and pointing at me? Why is she approaching me?* He did not recognise her and he began to wonder if she was approaching him for the same reason the locals had stared and exchanged hushed whispers about him in the convenience store. No one thought to stop her as she slowly made her way over to his table, her finger still outstretched as though accusing him of some unspoken crime. She was a few feet away when Tyler realised that he should attempt to flee, there was clearly something very wrong about this woman and he could not predict what she was going to do once she had reached him. Her pupils had become small black dots and the whites of her eyes seemed to glow with the essence of something otherworldly. It was something far more sinister than anything he had encountered on this plane of existence. Her mouth appeared to be trembling, it wasn't until she was merely a foot or two away that he realised she was saying something. She spoke faintly, each word was broken up but he could just about make out that she was saying, "you, it's you."

The waiter from earlier had approached her side and had placed a hand lightly on her shoulder, he tried to calm her down and get her to sit but she continued to stagger towards Tyler. He wanted so desperately to understand why it was that this woman was so terrified of him but he also wanted to leave and escape the horrifying situation. Her face was becoming contorted in an expression of pure terror.

"It's you, It's you," she murmured.

She had reached his table and in that same moment, Tyler realised that she hadn't been looking at him at all. He wasn't the one that she had been pointing at and he wasn't the reason for her hysteria. She was coming for Tara. Tyler turned to see how Tara was responding to this woman, but her expression was placid, she stared back at her as though unfazed by her strange behaviour.

"Tara? Do you know her?" Tyler managed to whisper, though she didn't answer him.

The woman was now standing beside Tyler, her finger almost in Tara's face.

"It's you, how did you do this? How? Sin, sin-" the woman seemed to begin to speak in tongues, bizarre noises and guttural sounds escaped her lips as her head rocked backwards and forwards. White foam began to appear in the corners of her mouth and her eyeballs twitched from side to side.

"Ma'am! Please sit down!" The waiter shouted at her as he attempted to ease her on to a chair.

The strange concoction of noises and words fell from her mouth in spasms of madness. Tyler had never seen anything like it. Her whole body was convulsing and sweating, her face had turned from white to blue and he was sure she was bound to pass out at any moment.

"YOOOOOO-UUUUUUUUU!" She screamed before thick black bile erupted from her stomach. It spilled all over their table, hot splashes hit Tyler in the face and he had to place his hand over his mouth to stop from himself from vomiting. The smell was horrendous - reminiscent of rotten meat and eggs. There were gasps and screams from the diners as the woman erupted once more, the chunky blackness took over the entire seating area yetTara remained still as it spilled all over her lap. Tyler quickly shot to his feet to stop any more of the vile fluid landing on him. The woman fell to the floor and began to violently convulse. Her arms and legs flexing and relaxing as though a powerful electric current was being sent through her entire body.

She emitted one last groan before her entire body went limp.

"Someone call an ambulance!" The waiter screamed as he fell to his knees beside her, "now!"

He placed his ear to her mouth and nostrils which were still plastered in the viscous black bile and waited a moment to see if there was any sign of life.

Horror flashed in his eyes and he immediately began to perform CPR. A few of the diners had come over to see what was happening and began to create a circle around them. Tyler was unable to move, the whole experience had rattled him and he had placed his shaking hands in his pockets to try and disguise exactly how much he had been shaken up by the reaction of this woman. The waiter continued to pump her chest and delivered mouthfuls of air through her lips which were already beginning to crust over with the black fluid. No one else offered to help, instead they stood around as though participants in some strange ritual. A few more moments passed and Tyler accepted the inevitable. The woman was dead. He turned to observe Tara. She had not moved from her seat, her hands were clasped over her lap and she watched on as the waiter tried to save the woman's life. There was nothing in her expression that conveyed any of the emotions that he or the other diners were experiencing. She was devoid of feeling anything and as he looked on at her, he knew there and then that this dead lady had known something was very wrong with this stranger who claimed to be his sister.

Chapter Seventeen

"You really need to let these wounds heal Lana. They're not looking too great," Rochelle pulled off her rubber gloves with a satisfying slap and disposed of them in a biohazard box. "I think we should report the incident to the cops, they'll have you sent to a more secure ward with someone watching out for while they can investigate what's going on. You can't put yourself at risk again."

Everything that Rochelle had said made perfect logical sense to Lana. This would have been the same advice she would have dispelled to one of her close friends but she couldn't apply it to her predicament. There was something telling her that as soon as she involved the law, the mystery surrounding her stalker and BlackButterfly would go cold and she would never uncover the truth of the situation. She knew her life was inevitably in danger but there was something that magnetised her to helping BlackButterfly. Lana felt that there had to have been a reason she had reached out to her and she knew that somehow she was the only one to saver her. Rochelle had been a great help so far and Lana was incredibly grateful for everything she had done. Rochelle had more than likely risked her job by doing everything as she had promised. She'd swiftly held off any further investigation by claiming that Lana's distress call was nothing more than an accident. She'd helped Lana to an unused medical room where she'd cleaned and stitched up the freshly opened gash in her abdomen. She had found some fresh hospital garments and instructed Lana to put them on.

"I know it sounds crazy, trust me but these things that have been happening... I think they've been happening for a reason," Lana explained as she pulled her night shirt back over her stomach, covering the freshly tended-to wound.

"It doesn't just sound crazy. It is crazy. That guy obviously wants you dead, he got in here undetected and if I hadn't got there in time, there is no doubt in my mind that he would have murdered you in cold blood." Rochelle shook her head, "I could lose my job over this. I have to do something, it just doesn't feel right-"

Lana grabbed Rochelle's hand, "please, you've done so much for me and I hate to ask this one last thing but I have to follow my instinct-"

"Yeah? And what about my instinct? Huh? How do I explain a missing patient who got away on my shift? How do I explain the damaged door in your room? What if they find traces of your blood?" Rochelle pulled away from Lana's hand and began to pace the room, "I really shouldn't have let it get to this. They'll no doubt be wondering where I am now!"

"You go about your normal duties, I'll trigger the alarm again and escape, it'll look like I damaged the door and made a run for it. You won't be blamed, no one will know any of this happened." Lana explained as she formulated the plan in her mind.

"There'll be CCTV footage or something, you can't get away with anything. As soon as you're reported missing, they'll launch an internal investigation-" Rochelle began to wring her hands as she spoke.

"Look, my plan is better at this point, if you report the incident now, they'll find out you lied about my distress call. That'll look worse." Lana said as she stood up from the bed.

"I'll just be honest. I'll say I wasn't thinking clearly-"

"I don't know any hospital that'll want to keep a nurse on staff that doesn't think clearly in an emergency," Lana said.

Rochelle immediately stopped pacing and put both hands on her head, "fuck!"

Lana approached her and placed an arm on her shoulder, "I'm sorry, I shouldn't have you got you involved and I don't mean to cause you any trouble. All I'm saying is turn a blind eye now and leave the rest to me."

Rochelle gently shook her head, "I really don't know about this Lana-"

"It's gonna be fine. Trust me."

"No offence but I don't trust anyone," Rochelle replied.

"Very wise, I get that." Lana nodded, "Look, just walk out of that door and go about your normal duties, I'll see to the rest."

"I don't know."

"Please." Lana squeezed her shoulder in the hope that it would infuse a particle of trust in her. After several tense moments of deliberation, Rochelle sighed and made her way to the door.

"Good luck Lana, I pray to God that I never see you again," Rochelle said as she reached for the door handle, "at least not here."

Just as she was about to leave, Lana called her name and Rochelle slowly turned, "thanks for everything," she said.

Leaving the hospital was easy. Lana returned back to her room, changed back into her civilian clothes and messed up the room a little bit more. She hoped it would look as though she had been angry and desperate to escape. Though a broken-down door might have seemed a little extreme, she knew that the hospital would have seen far worse especially in a big city such as New York. They already had her insurance details so there was no doubt she would pick up the bill for any damages - she considered it was a small cost to pay for getting out and finally discovering why she was wanted dead so desperately.

Once she had finished trashing the room as best as she could, she pulled the red emergency cord once again. The red light above her bed began to flash and she quickly left the room. She escaped through a fire exit at the end of the corridor and after navigating a few side streets and a parking lot, she was free of the hospital. She didn't know how much time she had before the police would get involved but she knew there was one place she had to go in order for the stalker to find her again. She had to return home but this time she would be more than ready for him.

*

The sun had peacefully descended below the horizon on the journey back to Cemetery Road. Tyler had watched the sky change colour from the passenger seat. At one point the entire sky was illuminated with a magnificent orange glow. If someone had told him that the universe had been set aflame in that very moment, he may have likely believed them. As the orange changed to a deep purple, a darkness began to invade the vast space around them, Tyler realised the atmosphere in the interior of the car was identical to that which was unfolding around them. Since watching the ambulance crew attempt and fail to revive the woman, Tyler and Tara had not spoken. They had no words as they watched the two young medical professions exchange a knowing look with each other and check their watches before loading the woman on a stretcher and carrying her out of the building. Tyler had cancelled their order and they left the restaurant in silence, however a thousand more questions had now arisen, the main two consisting of the identity of the woman, and what had she known about Tara that had sent her to her death. Tyler had overheard the ambulance crew make a preliminary assumption of her death as a heart attack, but he knew there was more to it. The way the woman's eyes transformed into nothing more than white shells, her violent expulsion of that putrid black bile and the way her body contorted and flexed before she uttered her final breath. He was unfamiliar with a heart attack claiming any victims in that manner. Something told him that Tara had incurred this horrifying event and Tyler was struggling to find the words to vocalise the mounting mass of questions he had for this woman claiming to be his sibling. Tara had said nothing. She had not communicated anything to say she was baffled or shocked by the incident, she carried the same expression that she had held at the table - passive and unaffected. He couldn't understand how she had remained so emotionless during the whole ordeal. They had stayed back briefly incase they were required for any statements, Tyler had given his contact details in case there were any questions and they were given the all-clear to leave. Tara had picked up her keys and left the restaurant without a second look back. Tyler had followed and got into the vehicle with her and she set off at a moderate pace. They sat side by side for the whole journey without a single word exchanged between them. It wasn't until they had returned home and had started to unpack the groceries that Tyler finally managed to muster up the courage to say something.

"Are we not going to talk about what happened back at the restaurant?"

Tara placed a couple of tin cans in the overhead cupboard and closed the door before she turned to him, "what is there to talk about?" She replied effortlessly.

"That woman. The way she was coming for you? Did you know her?" Tyler asked, trying his hardest to remain calm and controlled with his questions.

"I don't know what you mean?" She said.

"You don't know what I mean?" Tyler repeated.

"That woman had clearly lost her mind," Tara retorted, "that's all there is to it."

Tyler shook his head, "no," he started, "she saw you and it seemed to evoke something in her, it wasn't anyone else. There's was something about you that made her behave like that. Maybe it's because you're pretending to be someone you're not. Maybe she saw right through it, maybe-"

"That woman saw nothing. She was obviously having a nervous breakdown and lost it." Tara said as she began to unload another bag of groceries.

"So you just sit there and do nothing?"

"What was I to do?" Tara replied, "huh? Tell me? I'm all ears y'know."

"You could've done something," Tyler said.

"But I didn't. I could have made the situation a lot worse if I had participated in whatever hallucination she was having. I could have put myself and other people in danger. Did you ever think of that?" Tara slammed a carton of milk down and glared at Tyler.

He didn't know how to respond, he hadn't been prepared for Tara's defensiveness. "I guess not," he replied quietly.

"Look, it's a damn shame what happened to her, it really is but you're behaving as though I took a gun to her head and murdered her in cold blood."

Tyler lowered his head.

"Let's just forget this ever happened," Tara began to pull out pots and pans, "I need to get everything ready for tonight, my guests will be here in a couple of hours and I'll need you either out of the house for the night or upstairs."

Following on from her change of topic, Tyler offered to help.

"One hour and then you have to be out of sight," she answered.

Just a few days earlier, Tyler had been wondering where he life was heading. In fact, Tyler had a very good idea where his life was heading. It was heading nowhere. He had already determined that his life would have been over by this point, yet as he lay on the single bed in his woman's home - this woman who adamantly claimed to be his sister. This woman, who blatantly knew things only his sister would know. This woman with a secret in the basement and behaviour that seemed befitting in an entirely different dimension, he never could have predicted that this would have been the turn of events. A part of him felt a little relieved that he hadn't followed through and taken his own life. If his sister was in danger then he would stop at nothing to make sure that she was safe and sound - he at least owed her that. As he lay in the silence of the room, he wondered why he hadn't contacted the police. He knew the sensible option would have been to get them involved the immediate moment this woman claimed to be his sister. He had no recent pictures of her but he wondered if he could've demanded a DNA test. He wanted physical proof. Scientific proof. Anything that explained to him that this woman really was the same Tara Hamilton he had grown up with. Yet there was a conflicting feeling that seemed to offer a dull throb in his gut. A feeling that there was some connection with this woman and when she confessed to the murder of their mother, he knew that Tara was deeply associated to the flesh of this woman and he was worried that if he rocked the boat, the answers would disappear as the ripples expanded farther and farther outwards. Tyler knew that exposing the truth had to be done extremely carefully, something likened to the performance of a delicate surgery. One wrong move could prove to be fatal.

He had closed his eyes for only a moment but when he opened them, he sensed that there had been a change in the environment. He could hear voices downstairs. There was the soft beat of music playing and glasses clinking. *Tara's guests must have arrived,* he thought, *I must've fallen asleep.* He sat up on the bed and looked towards the door which he had left partially open. A warm glow beckoned through the gap and he tried to hone his listening skills so he could hear what was being said downstairs. It sounded as though there were at least five of six different voices chattering over each other at the same time. He was surprised that Tara had as many friends and he was further surprised that they were able to stop by and visit her in the middle of nowhere. Before he had retired to the bedroom, he'd helped her set out and prepare for the dinner party. Various dips were placed in serving bowls and refrigerated in advance, he had chopped an assortment of ingredients for a vegetable stew and opened several bottles of wine to allow them to breathe. There was no nothing unusual about the preparations for the party - no alters or sacrificial implements put out on display. In fact, the preparations bordered on tedium and something a lady of an older generation may have well put together. He'd half expected to set the table ready for several games of gin and have a large pot tea prepared for brewing. As Tyler stood by the door listening for any clues about Tara's guests, he got a sense of a presence elsewhere. It wasn't in the bedroom, it was coming from beyond the window. He turned to see the tops of the trees swaying gently against the backdrop of the night sky. A number of stars glittered and winked at him as he made his way over to get a better view. The moon came into view on the west side as he approached the window, it was full and round and exceptionally bright. It seemed closer to earth than he had ever experienced. Tyler glanced down into the garden and realised his instinct had been correct - stood in the far corner against one of the trees was a figure. He couldn't make out any of the person's facial features but the build and height revealed that the figure was most likely to be male. There was something odd about his posture. Tyler approached the window and squinted, he could make out that is was an older man with tufts of grey hair sticking out in various directions. *Who was this man and why was he standing in Tara's back garden? Was he a guest at the dinner party?* It became obvious that he had seen Tyler as he stepped backwards disappearing completely from view. Tyler spent a few more moments staring at the spot where he had once stood. Before he could conjure another handful of questions he felt his phone vibrate. It was Geoff.

"Hey, just stalking you- I mean, just checking in with you," he joked.

"Hi, it's probably not the best time," Tyler said very softly.

"Why are you whispering? Are you hiding in a closet?"

"Very funny," Tyler replied, "I wish it was that straight forward."

"I'm intrigued."

"I don't think that's the word I'd use," Tyler chuckled slightly.

"Well, as long as you're not in a life and death situation, I guess I'll let you go-"

"Before you go," Tyler interrupted, "can I ask you something? It might sound a little strange and I've tried to have a look online for an answer but I keep coming up dry."

"Well, people often refer to me as a fountain of knowledge, fire away." Geoff said.

"So, I'm visiting my sister and she lives in this tiny little village, I mean, there are about ten houses on this road and then miles and miles of fields surrounding us."

"Sounds cosy," Geoff laughed.

"Well, some of these houses have these symbols above their front doors. Like they're etched into the building itself," Tyler explained.

"Symbols? I'm not sure I follow?"

"Like, symbols I've never seen before. They reminded me of the runic alphabet but they don't match up, it's as though it's another language entirely."

"Sounds a little weird-"

"Right? I mean, that's not normal is it? It's not like a traditional thing that occurs in places like this?" Tyler questioned as he looked back out of the window again to see if the old man had returned. The previously occupied spot was still empty and a chill ran through his body.

"I've never heard anything like it, surely there must be a few answers online? You could try an image search, you might get a hit or two if you give that a go? Could you draw it from memory?" Geoff enquired.

"I took a picture. I have it on my phone."

"Even better. Send it to me and I'll have a look for you."

"You'd do that?" Tyler said, taken aback slightly by Geoff's eagerness to help.

Tyler heard a quick burst of laughter down the phone, "it'll take all of thirty seconds to search, I'm not gonna be writing a dissertation on it!" Geoff chuckled again.

Tyler felt a little embarrassed, "I know, I just didn't want to dump this on you."

"It'll be my pleasure to help."

"Thanks, I appreciate it." Tyler smiled, "listen, I'll have to get going. I'll send it now and we can speak later, okay?"

"Sure thing, Sherlock. You never explained why you were being so secretive?" Geoff asked.

"I'll explain later," Tyler said.

"Okay then, mystery man," Geoff laughed again, "you're an intriguing guy Tyler."

"I hope that's a good thing," Tyler responded, another smile had returned to his face.

"Oh, it's a great thing."

Tyler paused, he wasn't used to anyone being this pleasant to him since his break up, "well, I'll speak to you soon."

"No problem, have a good night," Geoff said.

"You too," Tyler hung up and opened up the gallery of pictures on his phone, he located the picture of the house with the strange symbol and selected the option to send to a recipient. However, just before he did so, something caught his eye. Something he hadn't noticed when he first snapped the picture. Tyler selected the re-size option and zoomed in to the window to the left of the entrance. It was mostly dark, nothing unusual but hidden just beneath the shadows was the unmistakeable image of a face. The further Tyler zoomed in, the quality of the picture began to diminish but the face resembled that of an older lady. Her eyes looked dark and sad, and she wore a shrivelled frown that emanated an overbearing sense of misery. Her stare matched Tyler's and he was reminded of images he'd seen of concentration camps during the Second World War, her expression would not have been out of place in some of those photographs. Another chill passed through his entire body causing him to physically shake. A creeping realisation that there wasn't just something wrong with Tara, but there was something very wrong with the people of Cemetery Road. Before he could allow the image of the woman's face haunt him any longer, he sent the image to Geoff and set his phone to silent-mode. Tyler knew that his next decision was most likely going to be a bad one but just as his instincts told him to look out of the window, they instructed him to gatecrash Tara's dinner party.

Chapter Eighteen

Bobby was sat in his usual position guarding the front desk and Lana knew that she couldn't make her presence known to him. She couldn't be sure whether the police department had notified anyone about her initial hospital admittance or if they were already on the lookout for her since her escape. Just as Rochelle had previously mentioned her distrust of anyone, Lana remained adamant that she would heed that same advice and avoid all interactions wherever possible. She had waited for over twenty minutes in a bitterly cold wind for a delivery man to arrive at the apartment complex. She was careful to ensure that Bobby was preoccupied with the signing for and storing of the deliveries to quickly sprint through the lobby and into the elevator. Her timing was impeccable as she managed to make it through without rousing any suspicion and she thanked all the Gods in the universe for the elevator door opening at just the right moment. It seemed that fate was on her side if only for those few split seconds. She didn't pass another soul as she slipped into her apartment, grateful that she had kept her house key stored in an inside pocket in her jacket and thus not stolen like her other belongings. As soon as she entered the hallway of her home and the amalgamation of familiar scents drifted towards her, she immediately felt better. The freshly stitched stab wound appeared to throb a little less and her thoughts became slightly clearer. However, the details of her plan remained somewhat foggy and as she attempted to formulate her next move, Lana began to realise how she was handling the situation in the worst possible way. She undoubtedly knew that she shouldn't be alone - it would only take a few moments to call Phoebe and have her pick her up but the determination for gaining answers outweighed all other sensible and reasonable options. Lana went straight to the kitchen and armed herself with a knife. She'd locked the front door out of habit but she had no doubt in her mind that her attacker would soon be making himself known and she was determined to be able to defend herself properly this time and on her terms. The apartment looked exactly as it had done when she left it, a white mug half full with cold coffee sat on the table next to her laptop. Lana wondered if Phoebe and Derek had come to see if she was home, she couldn't help but feel bad that she hadn't been in touch with them and let them know that she was okay. The truth was that she wasn't. There was still much to take care of and unfortunately, their peace of mind was way down at the bottom of the list. Without a second thought, Lana booted up her computer and logged back into Cassandra's Emporium. The main chat room flashed up on screen and a number of different messages appeared, she quickly scanned the names in the hope that BlackButterfly would appear. She didn't recognise any of the usernames so she typed her message and sent it into the chatroom.

Psychic_Orla: Hi I'm looking for BlackButterfly, are you here?

She watched the message fall into the stream of endless pleas for help and the other desperate attempts from fellow psychics looking to reel in prospective customers and prayed that she would get a response. The message was soon pushed off the screen and Lana felt her heart sink. She quickly typed another message.

Psychic_Orla: I'm looking for BlackButterfly, has anyone heard from her or know where she is?

Once again, the message dropped into the chatroom and was soon pushed out by all the other messages. Just as she was about to type another message, her computer beeped, signifying that she had just received a new direct message. Lana's heart began to race, *please,* she prayed, *please be her.* Without any further hesitation she clicked on the message.

ADMIN: HI PSYCHIC_ORLA, JUST A POLITE WARNING TO SAY THAT WE ADVISE ALL OUR PSYCHIC HOSTS NOT TO GIVE OUT OR REQUEST ANY PERSONAL INFORMATION, IN THE FORUM OR LIKEWISE, FOR SECURITY REASONS.

Lana felt like sending a strong worded reply back to the administrator but she couldn't risk being banned from the site. She decided not to reply and just as she was about to return to the main chatroom, the administrator sent another message.

ADMIN: HI PSYCHIC_ORLA, I THOUGHT I SHOULD LET YOU KNOW THAT WE'VE HAD A FEW COMMENTS ABOUT THE USER YOU ARE LOOKING FOR. SOME OF OUR HOSTS HAVE RECEIVED STRANGE MESSAGES FROM THE USER NAMED: BLACKBUTTERFLY. I ADVISE THAT YOU STEER CLEAR FROM ANYONE WHO COULD POTENTIALLY BREAK OUR TERMS AND CONDITIONS. PLEASE DO NOT PROVOKE OR PARTICIPATE WITH ANY USERS WHO MAY NOT BE USING OUR FORUMS FOR THE NEEDS AS IDENTIFIED ON OUR HOME PAGE. THANKS.

There was something about this second message that made Lana feel a little bit uneasy - the administrator was absolutely right. *If BlackButterfly was seriously in trouble, why had she not called for the police or sought help with someone she knew?* The realisation that she may have sucked into some sort of scam began to take hold and she began to curse for allowing herself to be played. Lana recalled the message that she had received from the other psychic who had warned her about responding to BlackButterfly and she started to think that there must have been a reason behind all the warnings. She replied to the administrator.

Psychic_Orla: Thanks. Do you know what she wanted?

She sat back in her chair and waited for a response, while she stared at the screen, she thought she heard a noise outside of the apartment. She listened more intently but was only met with silence, the stillness was soon interrupted by the beep of a new message.

ADMIN: HI PSYCHIC_ORLA, I DON'T HAVE ANY FURTHER INFORMATION ON THE MATTER BUT PLEASE REFRAIN FROM INTERACTING WITH ANYONE WHO MAY BE LOOKING TO BREAK THE TERMS AND CONDITIONS OF CASSANDRA'S EMPORIUM. THANK YOU.

"How could I be so stupid?" Lana said out loud.

She exhaled heavily and hovered over the button to log out of the site but stopped herself. She hadn't exchanged any personal information with Blackbutterfly, she had merely asked for her help and then not much longer after that she had been embroiled in the situation with the stalker. She couldn't justify escaping a hospital and surviving a number of stab wounds just to give up at this point. This girl had asked for her help and Lana was not about to give up without attempting to find out what the problem was. She flicked back to the chatroom once more and scanned the messages. There was still no sign from her, she scrolled back through the history to see if anyone had replied to her message. Lana scrolled further and further until she reached a notice where her message should have been.

ADMIN: THIS MESSAGE HAS BEEN REMOVED DUE TO A CONFLICT WITH CASSANDRA'S TERMS AND CONDITIONS. PLEASE DO NOT REQUEST OR GIVE OUT ANY PERSONAL INFORMATION.

"This is bullshit!" Lana cried out as she slammed her palms down on the table. "This whole thing is pointless," she felt tears begin to form in her eyes.

The computer beeped.

Lana lifted her head, her eyes blurry from the tears.

NEW MESSAGE FROM: BlackButterfly

*

Tyler had paced the room for what felt like a couple of hours trying to assimilate the information he had acquired over the last couple of days and how he should make his presence known at Tara's dinner party. His heart thudded in his chest as he played out a number of different scenarios. Unfortunately, all of them ended with Tara displaying her disapproval in a multitude of ways. He realised that he would just have to bite the bullet and see how her guests would react to him. After a few deep breaths and several silent wishes for a large glass of scotch on the rocks, he left the room and began to descend the steps. The music and chatter grew louder as he approached the downstairs area and his breathing was becoming more laboured. He kept practising his introduction in his mind, *hi, I'm Tyler, Tara's brother, it's nice to meet you. Hi, I'm Tyler, the supposed brother of this complete stranger who claims to be me sister. Hi, I'm the brother of this woman who knows my sister's deep, dark secrets, like the one where she murdered our very own mother.* He knew he would have to keep his introduction as brief as possible. He wanted to know more about her guests and the purpose of the dinner party. Further more, he wanted them all gone so that he could finally venture into the basement and find out what other secrets this woman was keeping. First of all, he wanted to understand the need for this social gathering and the reason why Tara had wanted him to stay out of the way. It appeared that all the rooms were occupied with people and noise and Tyler wasn't sure which room would be the best one for him to make his introduction. Tyler bit his lower lip and made his decision, he entered the living room. The conversations came to an abrupt stop as he stepped over the threshold and Tyler was suddenly aware of a number of different faces on him.

"Hello stranger, you look like a little lost lamb," an older lady wearing dark framed glasses and several layers of makeup spoke up. She swirled her glass of wine as she spoke and looked him up and down.

The room was occupied with eight other people, neither of them were Tara. They had all come dressed in formal evening wear and not a single one of them appeared to be under the age of fifty. The women seemed to outnumber the men, some of which sucked on cigars and drank what looked to be straight whiskey in ornamental glasses. There was a distinct sense of Tyler feeling un-welcomed and for a brief moment, he understood why Tara had asked him not to attend.

"Hi, I'm just looking for Tara, I'm her brother," Tyler answered, he tried to force a smile to appear as amicable as possible but the guests looked nothing more than confused.

"You're her brother?" The lady in the dark glasses asked before looking around at the other guests, her eyes wide in an expression of bewilderment.

"I guess she never mentioned me?" Tyler said.

The atmosphere had taken on a hint of humiliation and Tyler considered that it was most likely only himself that felt that way.

The other guests looked around at each other, as though awaiting for someone else to speak up.

Tyler broke the silence, "where is Tara?"

The question helped to diminish the overbearing hush and one of the men spoke up, "she's in the kitchen."

Tyler quickly thanked the man and began to make his way to the kitchen. He recognised Tara's voice before he entered and he stood by the door a moment.

"-the biggest sacrifice."

"You knew the risks though," another voice could be heard, it was another older woman's voice, this one appeared to be more frail and cracked when she spoke.

"I just don't know if I can do it anymore," Tara could be heard saying.

"Don't think about it," the other lady said, "shhhhhh did you hear that?"

"What?" Tara enquired.

"I think I heard something? Is there somebody there?" The old woman shouted.

Shit, Tyler thought, *she must've heard me listening in.* He knew there wasn't enough time to charge back upstairs and he had already introduced himself to the other guests so there was no way he could pretend that nothing had happened. He took another deep breath and stepped through the kitchen door.

"Tyler!" Tara shouted.

"I'm sorry, I'm sorry, I was starving-I was trying to go unnoticed," he answered as he held his hands up signifying that he surrendered.

Tara was stood by the counter preparing a tray of appetisers. Next to her was an older lady with long grey hair and a long multicoloured shawl hung over her crooked shoulders. Each body part appeared to be adorned with some form of jewellery. Bright jade earrings hung low from each ear and as she took a sip of her drink, her wrists rattled and clinked as a result of the countless bangles and bracelets that she wore. She was dressed less formally than the other guests, instead a loose floral cocktail dress peeked out from beneath her shawl, along with countless necklaces and vintage style pendants that were strung with brightly coloured beads and charms.

"Ah Tyler is it?" The old lady asked as she carefully walked over to him and held her hand out flimsily, the jewellery clattered as he shook it.

"Yeah, nice to meet you," he replied.

"And you too, I'm Reggie, though they call me Regina on a Sunday, but that's just between you and I," she smiled.

Tyler turned to Tara, she looked furious. Her cheeks had turned a rich shade of scarlet and her eyes had resembled knitting needles with their sharp precision. She seemed to be shaking slightly, a volcano on the verge of blowing its top.

"Tara, I'm sorry. I thought the kitchen would be empty," he lied.

"Has anyone else seen you?" She asked firmly, she had stopped preparing the appetisers and had turned to face him full on. She too, had made an effort, her hair had been pinned upwards in a neat bun, her eyes and lips accentuated with blues and reds and a long black dress, strapless at the back, clung to her skinny frame.

Tyler considered lying to her but knew that a roomful of people had already seen him and if one of them mentioned that he had introduced himself, his cover would be easily blown.

"I'm sorry, I got noticed when I came downstairs," Tyler answered as he watched Tara pick up an empty wine glass and launch it into the sink. Shards of glass exploded all over the kitchen and Reggie approached her to offer consolation.

"You have no idea, Tye. No fucking idea," Tara muttered under her breath and she turned to face the counter and shook her head.

Reggie wrapped an arm around her.

A pang of guilt suddenly hit Tyler hard, he was partly baffled by her reaction but also unhappy that he had upset her.

"Why is it such a bad thing? Are you ashamed of me or something?" Tyler didn't want to get too defensive but he couldn't understand her reaction, *who were these people? Why could he not participate?* Just like his whole experience in Edenville, nothing made sense.

The room fell silent and as much as Tyler wanted to charge over to Tara and physically shake the answers out of her, he knew it would do no good.

"I have an idea," Reggie said, "now that we're all acquainted, why don't we invite Tyler to dinner," she tapped Tara on the top of her arms and Tyler witnessed her whisper something in her ear. "What do you say Tyler? Would you like to join us for dinner?"

Tyler looked over at Tara who still had her back to him and her head hung down. There was no way that she could have offered him a inclination as to how to answer in her position, so Tyler shrugged his shoulders and replied, "sure. Why not?"

Chapter Nineteen

It felt as though Lana had waited most of her lifetime to receive a response from BlackButterfly. Seeing the message flash up on the screen caused the breath to get caught in her throat. Blood pumped forcibly through her body and her hands shook as she clicked on the button to open the message. Just as the message opened up, Lana heard another sound outside her apartment, this time it was as though someone had tried the handle.

"Not now," she whispered under her breath.

She quickly scanned the table to look for her phone before realising she no longer had one. She had no way of calling anyone. Her instincts told her to go and check on the door but she had BlackButterfly in her grasp now, she couldn't lose her again.

BlackButterfly: Hi Orla, how are you?

Lana was surprised by how casual her message sounded, like an old friend checking in.

Psychic_Orla: I've been so worried about you. I'm sorry our last conversation was cut short, my battery died and then I couldn't get hold of you again. Are you okay?

BlackButterfly: Not really, I could use help.

The front door rattled slightly, Lana tried her best to ignore it but panic was beginning to set in.

Psychic_Orla: Of course, how can I help?

She frantically typed.

BlackButterfly: Just promise me that you'll do what I ask but you mustn't ask any more questions? Please?

Lana recalled the warnings from earlier on and her initial desire to help was fading into doubt and expectations of being asked for her bank account details or other personal information began to emerge.

BlackButterfly: Do you have a pen and paper?

Lana stood up and pulled a pad of paper and a pen from the kitchen drawer before returning to the computer.

Psychic_Orla: Yes.
BlackButterfly: I'm going to send you some text, I need you to handwrite the text in a letter and send it to the address I will give to you. Can you do that?

The request had been far from what Lana had been expecting and part of her wondered if this was some sort of a prank.

Psychic_Orla: Sure... is that all you need?

BlackButterfly: Yes, just ensure that when you send the letter that it's not post marked from where you are.

Psychic_Orla: Okay. I'm not sure how I can do that but I'll try.

BlackButterfly: It's important.

Psychic_Orla: Okay.

BlackButterfly: Once you've sent the letter, please don't ever tell any one. It's important.

Psychic_Orla: Okay, but you're not in any trouble?

BlackButterfly: Please, no questions. Are you ready for the text?

Psychic_Orla: Yes.

BlackButterfly: *Dear Tyler,I wanted to say that I hope you are well and that life is treating you kindly. I've been thinking about you a lot recently. I moved a couple of years ago to a little town a few miles outside of the Lake District called Edenville. I've managed to rent a little house on a quiet street, it's surrounded by miles and miles of fields and greenery. I understand you must be busy but I was hoping that you would come and visit as soon as possible. I'd be delighted to show you around and* *catch up with you after all this time. It's been too long. Come and visit. Yours sincerely, Tara Hamilton*

*

Tara called the guests into the dining room and one by one they willingly came through and took their places at the table. Tyler had taken a seat in between Tara and Reggie and had poured himself a large glass of cabernet. As each of the guests entered the room, Tyler felt the same bemused looks cast towards him and he was reminded of how the people in the town and convenience store had looked at him previously that day. Tara guided them to their seats with a few wistful movements of her arms and a forced smile that Tyler could tell she was struggling to maintain. However, her mood had changed considerably since he had made his presence known and he wondered how her behaviour may have turned out without the support of Reggie. He attempted to put those thoughts to the back of his mind and concentrate on ploughing through the dinner party without any further disruptions. The guilt still clung to him and though he was aching for some answers, he got the sense that turning a crowd of people against him might not be the wisest of ideas. He took a few more mouthfuls of wine as the last of the guests took their seats. He observed a few of them offering brief whispers in their neighbours ears. The men had stubbed out their cigars and the women had freshly sprayed perfume and fixed their makeup. Each place was taken and Tara remained standing and waited for the chatter to die down before addressing the group.

"Good evening all and thank you so much for taking the time to come by," she began, "it's always a pleasure bringing us all together for these-" she paused, "events."

A few of the guests tapped the table with their wrinkly hands to offer their support.

"Thank you," Tara took a deep breath, "and I would like to take this opportunity to introduce my, somewhat, unannounced gust. This here is Tyler Hamilton and he will be joining us for dinner. I would hope that you can all join me in making him feel comfortable and at ease this evening," she said.

Tyler noticed her voice was beginning to waver slightly, her nerves seemingly getting the better of her.

"Tyler says that you're his sister?"

The guests turned to the older lady with the dark framed glasses who Tyler had spoken to in the living room previously. The room descended into silence and Tyler could feel his heart thudding against his ribcage. There was an air of aggression settling around the table and he was beginning to feel as though he had become stuck in a bear trap. He looked up at Tara who was having a hard time swallowing and keeping her hands steady. She picked up a glass in an attempt to occupy her feverish fingers and the silence hung in the air for a few moments more. He noticed she was blinking quite considerably, it looked as though she was trying to contain an overspill of thoughts and he felt slightly pained to see her this way, despite their previous conflicting talks. Without another thought, he rose from his seat.

"Hi," he began, all eyes immediately turned to him and he heard a slight gasp from Tara. "I'm sorry for the intrusion, I know this was highly unexpected for all of you as well Tara."

The room stayed silent.

"So, there appears to be a little confusion here, you see, I was travelling through this area and unfortunately got a flat tyre. It seemed to just literally explode right in the middle of the road. My phone battery died, you know how it is. right? Anyway, I had no way of being able to contact anyone so I just starting walking. God, it seemed like I was walking for a lifetime, these roads just seem to stretch on forever. I was hoping I would find a garage or at least somebody who might be able to help, but I had no luck." Tyler stopped and took a sip, the story was rolling off his tongue but he wanted to claim a few seconds to solidify the series of events in his mind so it appeared to be as true as possible. "Well, that was until Tara stopped by. She picked me up on her way home from shopping for this party. I didn't want to trouble her but I had no choice, I practically begged to use her phone to call for help but as it turns out, she hadn't brought it. I begged and pleaded that she help and out of the kindness of her heart, she gave me a ride back here so I could call a local garage. I would've been stranded if it wasn't for her. I'm extremely grateful for everything she's done." Tyler paused once more, the guests remained placid in their responses making it difficult for him to gauge whether or not they believed his story. "I asked if I could stay the night since the garage couldn't get out to me until the morning, so here I am," Tyler turned to Tara, her face was aghast but her shaking hands seemed to be slightly more under control. "Thanks again Tara. I owe you one." Tyler quickly raised his glass in her direction and took a seat.

The guests stayed silent a few moments more before Tara spoke up, "well, I'll bring in the starters," she turned to exit the room but was stopped by the older lady clearing her throat quite loudly.

"But I distinctly recall you introducing yourself as her brother? Am I right?" She adjusted her glasses as she spoke and offered a few glances around the table to see if anyone else would back her up on her comment.

Tyler felt his heart rate race again, *shit,* he thought, *I did introduce myself as her brother.* He forced a quick laugh to dispel the awkwardness that he was suddenly feeling. "I did, did I?" He said before forcing another laugh. "I guess I didn't realise I did that, I have many terms or endearment for people, I guess in a lot of ways what Tara did for me tonight was quite sisterly," he tried to joke. This newfound desire to protect her was not only baffling him but causing a great deal of stress. "Just to be clear, we've never met before, we're not related," he said, "I'm sorry if I've caused any confusion, that wasn't my intention at all."

"You've never met before?" The old lady asked, a wry grin started to appear on her face, the wrinkles growing deeper as it formed.

Tyler heard a few chuckles from the other guests, some placed their hands to their mouths to disguise their smiles, some looked down at their place mats. He couldn't understand what was causing such amusement.

"No, we've never met before," Tyler said a little more firmly, "like I said, she was kind enough to help me out this evening." He wondered how big a hole he was digging for himself, he partly wished he could dive right into it to escape the situation. His response was met with a loud burst of laughter from one of the other ladies.

"What's so funny?" Tyler asked, he was beginning to grow frustrated.

"Now, now," Reggie stood up and outstretched her arms to try and restore some peace, "let's all settle down, Tyler is a guest here and we should make him feel comfortable."

"He has no idea-" one of the guest started to speak before Reggie interrupted her.

"Like, I said, he is our guest tonight so we must remember how we treat our guests."

Tara seemed to nod slightly in agreement with what Reggie was saying, she was clearly not sharing the amusement of the other guests. In fact she looked ladened with worry. "I'll be right back," Tara said before quickly leaving the room.

"With all due respect Regina, you know we never have outside guests at these dinners?" The lady in the glasses piped up, her resilience was unwavering.

"Sometimes the rules are broken. Nothing changes, we carry on as normal," Reggie said.

"But we can't carry on as normal," another guest shouted.

"We carry on as normal," Reggie repeated, "we're just a little more-" she took a breath, "-careful."

Tyler noticed that she had cast him a quick glance as she lowered her tone on the last word. As much as he wanted to question what she had meant by 'being careful' he knew that he shouldn't turn on the one person that helped him diffuse the situation. He was going to sit quietly and observe, though he was glad that the lady in the glasses confirmed that he was not in fact losing his mind over this entire bizarre excursion. Something was clearly going on and this dinner party was obviously a cover for something much more sinister.

Chapter Twenty

The sounds at the door had stopped once BlackButterfly had sent her final message and Lana had used the next few moments to do as she had been instructed. She took a deep breath as she placed her pen down. Lana had copied everything that BlackButterfly had requested including the address the letter was to be sent to - though she was not sure how she would get it the UK without any identifying marks from where it had come from. There was also another address provided, a place called Edenville where this woman, Tara, appeared to be from. As requested, Lana hadn't asked any more questions, but she had developed a thousand more. Of all the requests she had predicted, this was one that she had not been prepared for. BlackButterfly thanked her for her help and signed off almost immediately. Lana had wanted to keep chatting to BlackButterfly but it was clear that she needed to leave, for reasons she didn't disclose. Lana's body seemed to buzz with adrenaline, her nerves snapped and sizzled inside of her as she tried to put the pieces together but nothing was any clearer. She had wanted to tell BlackButterfly about the stalker and her attack, she wanted to know if he had something to do with this whole mess and if her life was at risk for helping her. Yet, she had done everything this anonymous person had asked without questioning it, she sat quietly for a moment, wondering why she had felt so inclined to help. Her search for answers had been pointless. As Lana finally wrote the recipient's address on the front of the enveloped she wondered what sort of man Tyler Hamilton was. *Is he in danger? Am I putting his life in risk?* Lana stood up to try and shake away the questions and made an oath to herself, *I'll send the letter, I'll leave Cassandra's Emporium and I'll be done with this mess.* She accepted that she would be content with knowing that she had done everything she could. As she turned to head into the kitchen, she suddenly became aware that she wasn't alone. A chill kissed the back of her neck and it ran down the entire length of her spine. She hadn't heard any other noises whilst she had been so focussed on writing the letter. But something struck here there and then.

She felt eyes on her.

She felt *his* eyes on her.

Lana took a deep breath and spun around, she expected to come face to face with the stalker but she was met with an empty apartment. She scanned the rest of the room quickly before her gaze fixed on the doorway, more specifically the gap where the door had been left open slightly.

And then she saw him.

He stood motionless watching her. His eyes seemed to glow in the narrow gap between the frame and the door, he was otherwise surrounded by darkness.

Lana reached for the knife.

"I know you're here so you might as well show yourself," Lana called out, her mind was spinning with a number of different plans. This was what she had wanted. This was her opportunity to get some answers.

The door creaked open slightly and Lana got a better look of her assailant. It was the same man who had first showed up at her apartment, the alley way and the hospital.

"Come to finish the job?" She shouted, though she had previously been attempting to shy away from any attention, now she wanted to generate as much noise as possible with the intention that it would rouse suspicion and someone would perhaps call for help. She hoped that there would be enough time to squeeze a few answers from this man. As she studied his features, she noticed there was an emptiness not only behind his eyes, which occasionally flashed a green hue, but within him. He reminded her somewhat of a life-size puppet.

"You really don't speak much do you?" She shouted again, "what the fuck do you want? Huh?" She waited to see if he would respond but instead he stood motionless, continuing to watch her.

Suppressing her anxiety and and firing up her eagerness to fend for herself, Lana continued. "Are you deaf? What do you want, you asshole?" She had intentionally upped her volume by a few decibels and the man responded by taking a few steps towards her. He had figured out what she was attempting to do. He held a finger to his lips and she retaliated by screaming as loud as she could. The man looked shocked and lunged directly at her, tackling her to the floor. Lana screamed again and swiped the knife at him. She managed to get a clear hit in his collar bone and grimaced as she felt it make contact with the bone. He grunted but it didn't stop him.

"Get off me!" Lana managed to cry out before he wrapped his hands around her throat and began to squeeze. She felt the blood rush to her head almost immediately and began to kick and flail her arms about. The knife slashed into his body several times but he didn't seem to be affected by any of the blows, instead he continued to apply pressure to her neck. Lana spluttered and gasped for air, she could feel her stitches pulling at her skin and she knew that within a few moments they would be ripped out once again. Rainbow coloured spots formed in her eyes and a whole new level of panic set in. She flashed back to the incident in the alley and Lana was faced with the realisation that she was merely moments away from death. She knew she wouldn't so lucky this time around and the panic of losing the fight brought about one last surge of strength and she rose her arm, the same one that was still tightly clenching the knife and plunged it right into his face. The impact caused him to release his grip instantly and she gasped for air. Sweet air passed her lips and in that moment she wanted every inch of her lungs filled with luxurious oxygen. She knew she couldn't relish in that delight for too long and brought the knife up to his face again. He had his hands placed over his eyes to try and stop the bleeding but that didn't prevent Lana from slamming the knife through his left hand and into his skull. She heard the sound of air escaping followed by a deep gurgling noise. Blood spurted through his fingers and though it had been red previously, the more the blood pumped out from his face, the more it began to change colour. Lana pulled herself back and watched the red turn to a dark green. It flowed down his fingers and splashed all over the floor. She wanted to scream. She wanted to stamp up and down on the floor and shout out of the window, she wanted the entire apartment complex to know she was in trouble and take her away from the horrifying sight. Yet, no sound escaped her lips. She remained silent and in shock, watching on as her stalker used his hands to prevent any more blood from spilling out all over the place. It wasn't until he moved his hands away from his face that she finally managed to make a short high pitched shriek, she realised that his face had completely caved in, revealing nothing more than two loose eyeballs that hung just above where the lower part of his jaw remained. His nasal cavity was fully exposed and Lana observed his fleshy grey brain tucked away in the back of his skull surrounded by not only the green fluid but internal flesh that looked almost black. It reminded her of a slab of decomposed meat and she held her mouth to prevent herself from vomiting. The stalker emitted a loud wail and lunged at her once more. Before she could get away, he was back on top of her, his sticky hands wrapped around her throat once again. She looked up at his cavernous face and screamed as small lumps of flesh landed on her face. The cold meat slid down her cheeks and made soft thuds as it landed on the floor.

"No-ooooooo!" She managed to scream before the rainbow coloured dots began to reappear and she realised she was no long clutching the knife. Her only hope of survival was to use her hands this time. She reached up and forced both palms into the hollow shell of his head. Her fingers slid into the brain with ease, and just like the flesh, it felt cold to the touch and seemed to explode like she was popping bubble wrap. She squeezed her fists closed, ensuring that the brain was completely pulverised. Chunks fell into her face and mouth but she didn't have time to clear it away, she dug her fingernails into the back of his skull and with one last movement, she gripped on to as much of the internal gunk as possible and ripped it clear out. The sound of flesh tearing from bone was gut wrenching and her stomach turned as she threw it away from her. His grip on her throat lessened and the remainder of his head landed clear in her own face. Her voice had completely gone with all the previous screaming and though she wanted to scream and jump up away from the body and get as far away as possible, she found herself calmly pushing the bloody remnants off of her head. Lana sat up and looked at what was left of the stalker. He lay face up, his body mostly intact, despite a few stab wounds which bubbled with the dark green fluid but only the back part of his skull remained, loosely attached to his spine. There was something inhuman about what was left, where Lana would've expected to see reds and pinks inside the man. She saw blacks and greens. She struggled to comprehend exactly what it was that she was seeing but the sight confirmed that she was merely uncovering the tip of the iceberg. She rose to her feet and brushed off a few more pieces of brain matter and took one last look at the man's remains.

Just as she had felt so deeply inclined to help BlackButterfly, she now had a new motivation and it chilled her to her very core. She was about to embark on a deep sea diving expedition and find out what was below this proverbial iceberg.

*

Tyler helped collect the last of the remaining plates. He carefully stacked them on top of one another, interweaving the knives and forks in between them to prevent them from falling to the floor. The guests had returned to the living room for coffee and biscuits whilst Tara began to clear up in the kitchen. Tyler could hear the rattle of cutlery and plates as she tidied them away, he detected a sense of annoyance in each sharp bang and rattle. She was taking her frustration out on inanimate objects which Tyler was grateful for, he didn't wanted to be on the receiving end of those blows. He imagined she was cursing his name under her breath wishing that she had never let him step foot in her home. Tyler carried the remaining crockery through and placed it on the side.

"Can I help you wash these?" He asked.

Tara had her face buried on the inside of the refrigerator, her hand clenched tightly on the handle - her knuckles as white as bone. She took a step back and the light from the interior illuminated her face in a way that it appeared she had no distinguishable features.

"You've done enough," she replied coldly before turning back to place a plate of leftovers in the chiller.

Tyler started to make his way back to the kitchen door, "you know I did you a favour tonight. I don't know what it is that you're hiding or that you really are my sister-" Tyler stopped. "There's something that," he froze again and turned to look at her, her face was still focussed on the stacks of vegetables in the refrigerator. "I can't explain, it's like my sister is locked inside of you, I can feel her. I've felt her ever since that night. She's here, I know it and when you told me about what happened with mum well-" Tyler felt a lump in his throat. "Well, I knew with no doubt in my mind that Tara would never tell that story to anyone and the only person she could ever admit that to would be me."

Tara stayed unmoving from her position.

"Tara, if it kills me, I will get to the bottom of all this mess. This place, these people, these strange fuckin' symbols on these houses. I don't know what it all means and I don't know where my sister fits into this. All I know is that she would tell me. She would find a way of telling me what is going on and I would understand." Tyler took a breath. "So what I'm saying is, if you really are Tara, if you really are my sister then I beg you to do that one thing for me."

Tara finally turned away from the refrigerator, her eyes were red and wet, "do what?" She asked softly, the words seemingly difficult to speak.

"Find a way," Tyler said, "find a way of telling me what's going on. I'll work out the rest, I'll find a way to help, I'll-"

"Is everything okay in here?"

Tyler turned around to be greeted by an old man. He recognised the unruly tufts of hair on his head - it was the man that had been lurking in Tara's back garden. He pushed past Tyler and strode into the room, his face was ruddy and his eyes flicked furiously from side to side.

"Tara," he said firmly, "what's going on here?"

Tara quickly wiped her face and sniffled, "oh nothing Roy, I was just tidying up here, I was just getting ready to join the others, would you like to stay?" Her voice quivered with desperation and Tyler couldn't quite understand why Tara wasn't mad at him for just walking into her house uninvited.

"I guess you regularly walk into other people's homes?" Tyler asked him, standing defiantly in the doorway.

"Excuse me?" The man replied, turning back to face Tyler.

"You just walk in without even a knock at the door?" Tyler said, "seems quite rude to me."

Roy smirked and turned away, "who is this prick?" He asked Tara.

"Roy, don't." She said, her eyes moving to her feet.

"No, I'm curious. We don't have strangers here Tara, you know that."

"Roy, please-"

"Look, she helped me out, I'm leaving soon so what does it matter?" Tyler interrupted.

"Oh! She helped you did she?" Roy exclaimed and clasped his hands together feigning excitement. "Well this should be good." He turned back to Tara awaiting her response, but she stayed quiet.

"I didn't really give her much of a choice, I got a flat tyre, I needed some help and I wouldn't take no for an answer." Tyler said.

"Well-" he began as he took a few steps over to Tara and placed an arm around her, he brought her close to him and squeezed her shoulders tightly, "Tara's not one for giving no as an answer," he said as he winked at Tyler, "if you know what I mean?"

Tyler felt a revulsion in the pit of his stomach. He looked into Tara's eyes and he saw something else, a slight hint of fear. He fought back the urge of charging over and planting his fist firmly in Roy's face. In those few seconds, he wanted nothing more than to swipe the grin from his monstrous face.

"I think it's about time you left." Tyler instructed as he stepped aside from the door.

Roy laughed and took a step in Tyler's direction, "I think it's time YOU left," he said, "but something tells me that you'll be leaving much sooner than you think."

Tyler fought back the urge to respond and took another step away from the doorway to signify he wanted the man gone. Roy chortled and began to make his way out, just as he was about to depart, he stopped and without turning around spoke to Tara, "I'll see you later."

Tyler waited until he heard the front door close and approached Tara.

"What the hell was that all about? Is he-?" Tyler paused to figure out to phrase the last part of his question, "is he hurting you?"

Tara exhaled quickly and grabbed Tyler by his shoulders, "don't be silly, I'm fine, he's fine. He just gets a little- I dunno, defensive sometimes."

"That's not the word I would use," Tyler replied.

"He's fine, he's harmless," Tara began as she moved away from Tyler, "right, I really need to get these desserts out because I don't want them in the house once the guests have gone. Gotta watch my figure." She began to open and close cupboards and drawers.

"Hey Tara," Tyler said as he made his way to the door.

She paused and turned to him.

"Remember what I said," he whispered before leaving the room.

Tyler had returned back to the bedroom while the dinner party was still in full swing downstairs. He was equally furious and baffled, the incident with Roy in the kitchen had caused his blood to boil and though he wasn't a violent man, seeing the way that he behaved with Tara, he knew he would have had no problem with smashing his face in there and then, regardless of how old he was. Tyler had developed something of a skill at holding back from certain impulsive behaviours, he would always try and think two steps ahead and the consequences would not always be in his favour. He took a seat on his bed attempting to understand how his whole attitude towards Tara had changed. He had never thought that she might be in trouble, whoever she really was. *Perhaps she was using Tara's identity? Maybe she knew where Tara was but she was protecting her?* When he had seen how anxious she looked at the table, it struck him that maybe it wasn't Tara that was the villain. If the events of the evening had revealed anything, it was that Roy was most certainly not a good guy. His brain ached and he wanted nothing more than to get a good nights sleep. He still wanted to explore the basement and hoped that whatever was down there might bring the whole thing together. Tyler knew that he was clutching at straws - the chances of him getting to the bottom of whatever was going on by snooping in an old damp basement were quite slim. He recalled the strange music that he had heard down the other night, *there's something that she doesn't want me to see down there,* he thought. *There must be a reason for it.* Before he could formulate any more plans, he felt his phone vibrate, he pulled it out of his pocket and noted the time illuminated on the screen, it was just past midnight and Geoff was calling him.

"Oh hey! I can't believe I got through!" Geoff exclaimed.

"Hi, yeah it's five past twelve," Tyler replied, he felt himself smiling upon hearing his voice.

"I know, I know," Geoff started, "I've been trying all evening but the call just wouldn't connect at all, I was beginning to think the villagers had gotten to you!"

Tyler laughed softly, "you have no idea how accurate that sounds," he said, "I guess the reception's pretty crappy out here, sorry about that."

"It's okay, I just wanted to let you know that I did a search on those symbols you sent me-"

Tyler shuddered as he recalled the picture, the pale face in the window looking out at him. The forlorn eyes that looked as though they'd seen a thousand executions and he wondered if Geoff had seen it too.

"Oh yeah? Any luck?" Tyler replied.

"Nothing," Geoff answered, "I must have spent an hour or more running various searches on the picture, descriptions of the picture. I even went as far as doing some research in ancient languages. I never thought I'd be doing something like that for pleasure," he joked.

Tyler felt deflated from Geoff's response, he'd hoped for something that might offer a clue. "Well thanks for looking, I appreciate your help."

"It's my pleasure," Geoff replied, "so listen, is everything okay? I mean you sound, I dunno, kinda stressed-" Geoff stopped, "I'm sorry I don't mean to pry but I get a sense that something's up?"

"I'm just tired," Tyler said.

"I guess you're not used to random guys calling you at midnight then huh?"

"It's not something I'm used to," Tyler smiled.

"Well, don't let me keep you up. If you ever need to vent or just have a stupid chat, you know where I am," Geoff said.

"Thanks, I don't know why you're being so nice to me but I'll take it. I appreciate it," Tyler said, "and thanks again for being my private sleuth."

"Anytime handsome, anytime."

"G'night," Tyler hung up.

It felt good to have a moment away from his cascade of thoughts but the knowledge that there was no record of what the symbols on the houses meant caused him to feel deeply isolated. He knew that he was dealing with something that was intended to be kept very well hidden.

Chapter Twenty One

Lana had encountered a few creeps in her time. There was always the odd individual with a particular kink or desire and some of the situations she had found herself in had gotten a little bit prickly on occasion. This in turn meant that Lana had become quite skilled at two things; defusing a potential volatile situation and defending herself. As a precaution, she would always attend a job armed with a bottle of pepper spray stashed away in her handbag and a flip-knife that she kept hidden away in a concealed pocket in her jacket. She was not one to take too many risks though that had changed once she had encountered BlackButterfly. As she dragged what was left of her stalker's body to the bathroom, she thought about the many times she had had to fend for herself. On one occasion, she had met up with a middle aged man who was incredibly charming and chivalrous at the beginning of the evening. He'd pulled out her chair before he had taken a seat at the restaurant and insisted that she request her beverage first. However, when she witnessed him drop something in her champagne as they had drinks in the hotel bar, she knew that he was nothing more than a low-life scum bag who didn't actually care for her as he had so carefully pretended in the beginning. He wanted to do unspeakable things to her without her consent and she wasn't going to let him get away with it. She whipped her phone out, snapped a picture of his pathetic face, slammed her pointed shoe in between his legs and told him that if he ever thought about doing what he had intended to anyone else, she would happily take his mugshot to the police. He'd fallen on his back as she had threatened him and she didn't care that the whole bar had turned to see what was happening. He called her a bitch and she walked out of the hotel without a single look back. Lana was stronger than she believed she was and as she cut up the stalker's body in her bath and scrubbed the stains off the floor, she kept her head held high and her wits about her. She had done what she needed to do and she knew she should've reported it, she should've gotten someone else to investigate where this man - this strange creature came from and what he wanted. But Lana knew that after days of questioning, the case would be taken out of her hands, she would go back to living her normal life and the discovery of this otherworldly being would be swept under the carpet. She didn't want it to end there, she could potentially unlock one of the world's biggest secrets and expose it to the world. Whether this was a new species, or another life-form, she couldn't be sure. All she could be sure of was that the possibilities were infinite. Lana had always had a sense that there was more going on beneath the surface. There was more to the mind-numbing humdrum of everyday life and she was ready to pierce the veil. Perhaps this had been her calling and the true reason she had decided to stop escorting. *Perhaps this was all happening for a reason*, she thought to herself.

As she snapped the bones which were strangely very brittle and cut away the flesh, she realised that the creature was physiologically as human as could be on the outside, but told an entirely different story internally. She had only every studied anatomy at high school, so she had a very basic knowledge of the topic but she knew that a living organism should have internal organs. This creature was made up of nothing more than bones which would break and bend like plastic, a dark fleshy material and a circulatory system with no pump. She could not find a heart inside the thing - she couldn't explain how the blood circulated its body. As she started to heave the body material into black bin bags, it occurred to her that perhaps the body was just for show. An avatar used to walk amongst other people without getting recognised for what it truly was. Except she had noticed something, a green glint in his eyes. She had seen it a few times. The thought that there could be more of these things walking around pretending to be human caused a shiver through her body. *I really can't trust anyone,* she realised. An even more terrifying thought occurred to her, *if these things could masquerade as any human, they could very well be people in power, politicians, FBI, doctors, scientists.* She put her hands to her head as if to prevent any more of these horrifying thoughts entering her brain. There was an overwhelming sense that she had unlocked something truly life-changing and she had the very proof in her own apartment, albeit cut up into small pieces and dispersed into a number of different bin bags - she still had the evidence all around her. As she tried to collect her thoughts and plan out her next move she heard a voice in close proximity.

"Lana!"

It was Phoebe.

An immediate sense of relief descended upon her and her instant response was to burst into the hallway and embrace her best friend. She wanted someone to hold her and tell it was okay, she wanted to unburden herself of this whole nightmare but she caught sight of her reflection. Her clothes were stained from top to bottom in chunks of guts and spatters of blood. She hadn't washed the dried mess from her face and it became apparent that her situation might not be fully believed, even by her best friend. Another thought came to her - *what if she is also one of them?* Lana tried to shake away the creeping sense of paranoia but she had no way of knowing for sure. Not unless she did what she had done to her stalker. Without another thought, Lana swiftly locked the bathroom door, undressed and dived into the shower. She turned the water on full power and began to scrub at her skin, observing the brown water wash down the plug hole. A moment later she heard knocking at the door, Phoebe's voice was just outside the door now.

"Lana? Is that you? Are you in there?"

Lana left the shower running while she pulled all the bags to the corner of the room, loading them with her filthy clothes on top and covering the entire pile with clean towels. She heard Phoebe speaking to someone else outside the door.

"Well, can't you just smash the door down? Do you not have a master key?" Phoebe asked.

Lana heard another voice murmur something, she recognised it as Bobby's. *Fuck,* she thought. She tried to recall if there was any more evidence left in the living room but she distinctly remembered telling herself to move everything to the bathroom and cleaned everywhere else first. She flicked the shower off and looked in the mirror breathing a sigh of relief to discover there were no remnants of dead bodies upon her.

"Time to play the role," she whispered to herself. "Hello? Is someone there?" Lana shouted.

"Oh my God, Lana is that you? Let me in?" Phoebe called through the door.

"Phoebe! Hang on a sec, let me get a towel, I was just in the shower," Lana called back, trying to keep her voice as care-free as possible.

"Are you serious? Let me in, I've been worried sick about you!"

Lana wrapped a large towel around her making sure that there were no stab wounds or stitches on display.

"One sec Phoebe!" Lana shouted as she quickly scanned the room. There was still blood spray on the tiles by the bath and bloody footprints on the floor.

She knew she'd have to keep entry to the room off limits. Lana opened the door slightly and pushed herself through the gap before closing it behind her. Phoebe grabbed her and squeezed her tightly. Bobby was stood at the far end of the hallway, looking a little embarrassed.

"Oh my God Lana!" Phoebe screamed, "you're okay!"

"I'm fine Phoebe, you're acting as though you've not seen me in a couple of years," Lana joked and faked a laugh.

"It's good to see Miss White, I'll leave you two now," Bobby said before departing.

Lana waved at him and then squeezed Phoebe into her, it genuinely felt good to see a familiar face.

"What's been going on Lanny? I had to file a missing persons report on you, the last time we spoke you were raving about some guy that was after you. The police said that a woman matching your description turned up at the city hospital, she'd been attacked or something and then escaped. The day they told me about her, I was on my way down to find out she had just left. She's been stabbed like a voodoo doll or something and walked out of the hospital! Can you believe it? God, Lanny I was so worried it was you-"

"Phoebe, breathe. First of all, I'm fine. I lost my phone which is why I've not been able to get in touch, I'm really sorry. I took up a very last minute escort job. It was a little high profile so I couldn't tell anyone anything, you understand?" Lana lied.

"Yeah - I guess - I thought you were giving up on the escort jobs... and the way you left that day-" Phoebe started.

"I'll admit, I was a little spooked but it was all for nothing," Lana said, she felt Phoebe's grip on her tighten and for a brief moment, she thought she saw a flash of green in her eyes.

"What's up Lanny?" Phoebe asked, her fingers squeezing into her arms.

"I could use a drink, what about you?" Lana asked as she started to move away from Phoebe and towards the living room.

"Yeah, sure. I guess-"

Lana led Phoebe through the doorway that only a few hours ago had been the very spot her stalker had watched her from.

"This place is a mess!" Phoebe exclaimed, "the floor's all wet?"

"Oh yeah, I spilled a drink before, I haven't had a chance to tidy up since I got back," Lana said as she grabbed two clean coffee cups from the draining board.

"When did you get back? Where have you been?" Phoebe asked as she took a seat on the arm of the sofa, Lana noticed her eyes were scanning the apartment and she prayed that there was no sign of the bloody murder that had occurred earlier on.

"A few hours ago, I was gonna call round to yours after I'd cleaned up," Lana said as she switched the coffee machine on.

"Smells weird in here," Phoebe commented.

"Yeah, sorry about that, like I said, I've not had chance to sort this place out."

"Your front door had been tampered with you know?" Phoebe said, her eyes were starting to bear through Lana.

"My bad, I forgot my key-" Lana started, surprised at her quick ability to cover her tracks.

"Look, something's going on. You don't disappear for nearly a week, lose your phone and key and just don't tell anyone where you are?" Phoebe said, her tone was beginning to get heated, "did you hear what I said earlier, I filed a missing persons report for you. A fuckin' missing persons report! No one knew where you were! Do you know how insane that is?"

"I know, Phoebe, Jesus - I'm really sorry, I really am. You know what my job can be like sometimes, the secrecy, the spontaneity," Lana began to explain.

"Escorting is not a fucking career path Lana!" Phoebe snarled.

Lana was taken aback by her outburst, "I'm okay. I promise you," she said.

Phoebe took a deep breath, "I don't know if I can believe you."

"I have no reason to lie to you, you're my best friend, you know that," Lana forced a smile.

Phoebe grew quiet, "can I use your bathroom?"

Lana's heart began to race, there was no way someone could enter the room and not notice the blood stains and the pile of body parts in big trash bags stored in the corner.

"Ah, did I not mention? I'm having plumbing issues with the toilet, I keep meaning to tell Bobby to report it to the maintenance guy-" Lana started.

"I just wanna freshen up, it's okay. I'll be back in a minute," Phoebe said as she rose to her feet and started towards the door.

"shit, shit, shit," Lana muttered under her breath and quickly ran after her, "Phoebe, don't go in there, please!"

As Lana exited the living room, she saw Phoebe standing at the entrance to the bathroom, she had opened the door, and though Lana could only see the back of her head she could picture her expression - her mouth wide open and the blood rushed away from her face leaving her ashen and clammy.

"Phoebe, I know this seems totally crazy-" Lana started, Phoebe turned around and once more she was sure she saw a green flash in her eyes. It lasted a second but she was sure she saw it. "You, you're-you're one of them aren't you?"

Phoebe stood motionless, Lana could see that one of the towels had fallen from the pile revealing a trash bag with a whole foot exposed from a tear. She knew this was going to be very difficult to explain. Before she could think of anything more to say, her instincts took over. Her skill of attempting to diffuse the situation hadn't worked on this occasion, so she knew would have to put her second skill to practice and defend herself. She leaned down and picked up the large stone door stop that was shaped as a cat and charged at Phoebe. She rose her hands as Lana slammed the heavy stone against her skull. She watched her friend's eyes roll backwards as the back of her head cracked against the bathroom sink and she landed on the floor like a doll that had been thrown from a high rise building. Her legs jutted out in obtuse angles and Lana looked down at her as blood began to pool around her head. She waited to see the blood change colour as it had done with her stalker, yet it stayed the same. A horrifying realisation crept over Lana as she watched the blood pool around her friend's body - she wasn't a monster at all.

*

Tara chased Tyler through the woodland. It was the middle of August and the days were at their longest and scented with wafts of freshly mowed grass. His legs ached as he darted through the trees but he giggled with the anticipation of being caught. It had been a game they played often - who could catch who? It was a few days after Tyler's sixth birthday and though he hadn't gotten his Birthday wish of a normal family, in that moment, he couldn't have been happier.

"I'm coming to get you!" Tara had shouted through the trees and the thrill of being caught caused adrenaline to pump through his body and generated a little more extra strength in his leg muscles - accelerating him forward like a chased cat. It was cool beneath canopy of the trees and the occasional beam of sunlight would flicker through the gaps like enticing golden ropes to heaven. He could hear her footsteps gathering speed behind him.

"It's not fair!" He shouted, "you're bigger and faster!"

He was quickly running out of breath so he stopped with his back to a tree. He heard her footsteps slow down, she knew he was hiding and his heart raced with the anticipation of being caught. A twig snapped to his left and as he slowly turned his head, an arm came from around the other-side of the tree and tapped him on the shoulder.

"Tag! You're it!" She called before she ran past him.

"Not fair!" He shouted back but she had gone.

Sometimes, she would let him catch up to her, other times, she took pleasure in winning. "You can't win them all," she would say. Sometimes, they would sit by the stream, gathering their breath and resting their weary leg muscles and Tyler felt a happiness in that moment that he had not shared with anyone else. It was a bond unlike anything he had experienced with anyone else and as they watched the sunlight reflect off the water, they made a promise, sealed with two interlocking pinkie fingers.

"Friends for life," Tara would say.

"Friends for life," Tyler would repeat.

He was suddenly brought out of his memory with a flood of anxiety in his chest, *did I fall asleep?* Tyler glanced at his watch, it was just before three a.m. He looked over to the door, it was dark so he presumed the guests must have left. He quickly rose from his position and crept to the upstairs hallway to be sure that there was no sign of life downstairs.

Silence.

Tyler looked over to Tara's room, the door was almost closed and he could make out that it was dark inside. He knew this was now his opportunity to see what it was that Tara was hiding away in the basement. Floorboards creaked as his tiptoed down the stairs, one by one. The air smelled of stale cigarettes and alcohol, and there was still the dull buzz of energy that tended to linger in the atmosphere after a gathering of people had got together that wouldn't begin to dissipate until the very next day. He carried on through into the kitchen and over to the refrigerator. Reaching up, his fingers brushed against something, he tried once again and the key fell to the floor. The sound as it bounced from one end of the floor to the other seemed deafening in the silence and he clamped his eyes shut, hoping that he hadn't awoken Tara. Clutching the key, he inserted into the lock, it jangled slightly as his hands shook. *Why am I so nervous?* Tyler tried not to entertain the question with an answer as he knew that there were countless reasons why. He heard the click as the door unlocked and he pushed it open. An elongated creaking noise came from the hinges and his eyes immediately caught sight of something. The door opened to reveal a set of wooden stairs with cracked walls on either side leading down into the basement. A faint glow game from the left corner. His eyes met the silhouette of a figure standing completely still at the bottom of the stairs. It was difficult to assess whether they were male or female but it didn't matter, his heart was racing as he emitted a faint, "hello?"

There was no response.

He had a momentary vision of the silhouette springing to life and charging up the stairs towards him but it didn't move. He called out a little louder this time, hoping that whoever it was that was down there would identify themselves. A few more moments of silence passed and Tyler began to debate whether he should just run away and leave this house altogether but the urge to know the truth about his sister was too strong. He reached for a light switch and as he did, the silhouette calmly walked out of view. He began to question what he had seen was real or merely a flicker of the shadows. Tyler felt around the wall but could not locate a light switch, he gave up and began to descend the stairs. He resisted the urge to call out again. Each step creaked in the same way the door had, as if they were calling out to alert Tara that he was on the verge of discovering what she was keeping locked away in the basement. The air grew cooler as he made his way down, by the last step, he was able to see his breath leave his mouth in small clouds of vapour. He wrapped his arms around his upper body and braced himself as he turned the corner.

The light was generated by a number of different candles and lanterns that had been placed around the room. Tyler observed an old sofa couch positioned in front of an old chest of drawers. Both of which stood in the centre of the room. He cast a quick glance around the rest of the room to see if he could see the silhouette-person hiding in one of the corners. The room was mostly empty despite the odd piece of furniture and junk stored away by the walls. It was what was atop of the chest of drawers that grabbed Tyler's attention. He took a few steps closer and discovered that there were a number of different artefacts placed on top of the large chest. Candles had been carefully positioned on the four corners, they had been reduced to small waxy stubs indicating that they had been lit for quite some time. Contained within the invisible parameters set out by the flickering candles were toys, more specifically - girls' toys. There were old dolls with a few strands of hair left sticking out of their otherwise bald plastic heads, foam ponies and horses, a small pram with a miniature porcelain baby placed inside. There were numerous other toys on display and Tyler realised that they had been placed in a circular formation around a picture frame. A small face looked back at him. Her sparkling blue eyes projected life and fun with just one look. She clung on to a teddy bear and she smiled exposing her missing two front teeth. Tyler leaned in closer to the picture, the girl with blonde hair tied up in perfect pigtails looked back at him, her innocent features revealing no clues as to why her photograph had been made the centre piece in the basement of a strange woman who was claiming to be his sister. He scratched his head - none of it made sense, but he could be sure of one thing. The arrangement of items on the chest of drawers looked very much like a shrine to this little girl. As Tyler scanned the room once more, he spotted a door at the far end. Before he could approach it, his pocket began to vibrate. He pulled out his phone, it was Geoff.

"I'm so sorry it's ridiculously late," he said, his tone was rushed and Tyler detected a sense of urgency in his words.

"It's okay, I'm up anyway," Tyler replied, keeping his voice low as to not attract any attention, "everything okay?"

"I don't know-" he started, "I've been up all night, I was gonna call you in the morning but I just couldn't sleep. That symbol-" Geoff paused and took a sharp intake of breath.

"Yeah, did you find out what it meant?"

"Not exactly."

"What do you mean?"

"So, after I couldn't find anything with my initial search, I thought I'd try again tonight and see if I could help you out," Geoff stopped, "I guess I was trying to impress you-" Tyler smiled slightly at his gesture and noticed he sounded a little embarrassed. "I started to research if anyone else had reported seeing strange symbols and I came across this forum, you know one of those places online where you can ask a question and anyone can send you a reply. The thread is kept live so if someone else has the same question they can find the answer from that particular conversation."

"Yeah," Tyler replied.

"So, I think I found a post from someone who had found something similar. The original poster claimed that he was travelling through a small town in Denmark and came across a village containing some buildings that had symbols etched in their entrance ways. He wasn't able to take a picture but he describes what they looked like and they match the symbol that you sent me Tye."

"They do?" Tyler was beginning to wonder whether or not he wanted to know what they meant. As he held the phone to his ear, he got the distinct feeling he was being watched. He scanned all areas but did not notice anyone.

"So, the guy who posted in this forum asks if anyone else has come across anything like them and he got a reply." Geoff took another breath and Tyler could feel his chest tightening. "Their English wasn't particularly great but the person who replied explained that these symbols represent the residence of a guardian, I hope I translated it okay but he goes on to say that the symbols are to inform those of where these so-called guardians live but to also warn them not to trespass on their territory otherwise-" Geoff trailed off.

"Otherwise?"

"It results in the death of the trespasser." Geoff finished.

"I don't understand what any of that means?" Tyler replied.

"I think it's some old ancient tradition or something, I don't think that it means anything now. Y'know, like small town folklore."

"I've never heard anything like it before," Tyler said.

"There's something else," Geoff uttered quietly.

As Tyler opened his mouth to reply, he heard a creaking sound. It sounded like the basement door at the top of the stairs. His eyes darted around the room looking for a hiding place.

"What?" Tyler whispered down the phone as he rushed over to door at the far end of the room. He presumed it was a storage closet.

"I don't know if I translated it okay-" Geoff began.

Tyler heard the volume of the creaking steps increasing, whoever was coming was about to reach the final step and turn the corner, he would be caught.

"What?" Tyler whispered with frustration as he grabbed the doorknob of the storage closet and pulled, praying that it wasn't locked. It opened swiftly, his eyes struggled to adjust to the darkness inside but as he stepped within and pulled the door closed, he realised it was much colder than the main basement area. He heard one last creak and footsteps and someone turned the corner and entered the room. He held his breath, afraid that his heavy breathing would give away his location. Beads of perspiration trailed down his forehead and rested just above his eyebrows. He pressed the phone against his ear, hoping that Geoff's voice wouldn't be audible to whoever had just joined him in the basement.

"If I translated it okay, then whoever had sent the reply had mentioned that the guardians were not human. They were demons."

As Tyler sucked in a mouthful of cold air in response to hearing that word, he felt an icy grip on his shoulder.

Chapter Twenty Two

Shallow breaths.

Slow inhale.

Slow exhale.

A darkness that seemed to carry weight, a force pressing down, lungs working extra hard to inflate with sweet oxygen.

Slow inhale.

Slow exhale.

At first there was just the sound of breathing, the instinctual process of gaseous exchange. Soothing and familiar. Though the sound was distorted almost as though it was being emitted thousands of miles below the ocean. Yet there was something else. Other noises - distant at first but with a little more focus and a little more concentration - they began to take shape. These sounds were less organic than the rhythmic breathing. They seem to pop and whistle. Further exploration of these sounds revealed that they were a little more developed, the pops became beeps and the whistles became static. Their signatures became more pronounced and there something else. A great amount of discomfort. Though she could not see, she could feel what felt like a thousand wires invading her body.

What have I done? She thought to herself. What have I done?

*

Tyler quickly span around and dropped his phone. He heard the sound of the screen cracking and instantly knew that it was beyond repair. The worse realisation was that he lost his connection with Geoff and any means for rescue. His eyes met another pair of eyes - her pupils flicked left to right like the ball-bearings on Newton's Cradle. Her hair was matted in thick clumps and stuck to her perspiring face which was smudged with what looked to be charcoal and dried blood. She pressed a single finger to her lips, and although Tyler had been silenced by the shock already he did as she instructed. He noticed that her clothes which looked ragged and filthy matched her dirty hands and face. He wouldn't have been surprised if she revealed to him that she been living in a cave in the woods. *Who was this strange woman and why was she hidden away in a storage closet in the basement?* At the very same moment that the thought presented itself in the forefront of his mind, he realised that he was not in a storage cupboard. Behind the girl, his eyes followed a long dark corridor. The walls were uneven, constructed of exposed rock as though it had been freshly dug by some very hardworking miners. He was suddenly flooded with questions but before he could entertain any, he heard footsteps begin to approach the door. The girl grabbed him by the shoulders and pulled Tyler back as a light tapping noise could be heard.

"Roy? Is that you?"

Tyler recognised Tara's voice - or at least the woman who was masquerading as his sister. He felt an impulse to rip the door off its hinges and shake this woman until she confessed what she had done to his sister but the girl with the icy fingers held him tightly.

"Roy?" She called softly again, and then, "Tyler?"

His heart began to pound, his ribcage close to exploding. The girl behind him whispered, "don't answer," in his ear. Her cold breath matched her freezing fingers.

Tyler couldn't explain why he found himself following her instructions but he believed he saw something in her eyes that was in sync with how he was feeling. After a few more foreboding moments where Tyler expected the door to be pulled open and his hiding place revealed, the footsteps could be heard retreating and he let out a sigh of relief. Pulling away from the girl, he turned to face her.

"Who are you?" He kept his voice low and hushed.

"It is you, isn't it?" The girl asked, her stare was slightly softer this time and despite the darkness, he could tell that tears had began to trail down her face. "Tyler, right? It really is you?"

"How do you know me? Who are you?" Tyler asked, his voice slightly more raised this time as a result of his growing frustration.

The girl pulled him down the corridor, "not here," she whispered.

Tyler stepped away from her grip and stopped, "I just want some answers!"

"I have them. i have them all, just follow me - it'll help if you see it."

Tyler began to feel dizzy, the weight of all the questions, the lack of any real rest and the fear were becoming all too much and he had to prop himself up against the wall with one hand.

"Are you okay?" The girl asked as approached him and placed a hand on his back. He shivered at the touch.

"You're so cold," he said.

"I know," she replied. "I'm sorry about all of this."

It had been a long time since he had received any words of comfort, never mind an apology. Her words seemed to soothe him and he managed to find the strength to stand on his own. He explored her face, she looked to be in her mid twenties despite large black circles around her eyes and the odd worry line creasing the top of her nose and corners of her eyes. He knew that this girl was attractive behind the dirt and the cloud of anxiety she carried with her.

"Who are you?" He asked.

"My name's Lana, now come on, we've not got much time."

Chapter Twenty Three

Wires protruded from the skin in all directions, surrounding her in an aura of multicoloured threads - she had become a marionette permanently attached to its strings. Thousands of these worm-like cables ran through her arms, legs, torso but the majority of them were embedded into her skull. Despite her inability to see exactly what sort of state she was in, she knew that the wires had been threaded through the bone and deep into her brain. It took a while for her to muster up the strength to open her eyes but when she did, she wanted to scream. A feeling of pure dread ran through the entirety of her body and the first thought was one that sent her spiralling into panic. *I should not be awake.* She could only align the feeling with that of waking up on an operating table during a very serious procedure. Except there were no scalpels slicing through her skin, there were no face masks or the rhythmic beeping of a life support machine in the background.

Her view was of something else entirely.

There was a foreboding darkness - a gloomy shadow that seemed to descend upon her perspective of the area but she could see that there were others. She could only presume they were like herself in the way that they were strung up by wires and tubes connected to various body parts. It was a large room and there were rows of bodies, and though she couldn't turn her head, she knew that she was sandwiched between a number of these similar bodies. All were held up in similar positions with hundreds of wires feeding into them. The bodies had been stripped down to their underwear and appeared to be breathing on their own. A young man could be seen just opposite her, his head hung low and his arms were pinned up in a crucifixion pose, unlike the rest. There was something happening with him, she noticed that there was some sort of movement occurring but she couldn't be too sure what it was. As she continued to watch, she tried to remember her name - the details were fuzzy, as though waking from an intense deep sleep. She tried to force the memories to come back to her and she squeezed her eyes shut in an attempt to regain some focus or infuse an image in her mind that would bring it all back. The next moment brought a flash or memories, who she was, why she there and her stomach turned over. The barrage of everything flooded through her and though it came with a greater understanding, she knew that there was something missing. A large part of her was missing. Her flash of realisations was broken by the sound of a loud crack and a deep groan. She flicked her eyelids open to see the young man's body twitching. The wires flapped with the convulsions of the body, tapping furiously against the floor and the apparatus that held him up. The other bodies seemed completely unaffected by his condition, remaining motionless with their heads hung low. She watched in horror as his head slowly lifted up and she heard another loud crack. Something inside of him was snapping and she wanted to run, but her body would not respond to her thoughts so she was forced to remain still - a stationary onlooker to the horror that was beginning to unfold in front of her. The man's jaw began to open, slowly at first and then it cracked as the jaw bone unlocked and the lower section began to descend towards his chest. The inside of his mouth was dark and cavernous, there was something deeply inhuman about the way it expanded. The skin around his mouth cracked and began to tear, blood seeped from the expanding wounds and she wanted to scream, she needed to be freed from this nightmare. *This was not what she had agreed to* - she remembered now - *this was not what she had wanted.* The young man's mouth tore wide open and his lower jaw was ripped clean from his face and landed on the floor with a hollow thud. Something began to crawl out from the back of his throat. She observed in catatonic terror as the seemingly dark and shiny thing made its way out of the man's mouth. In that same moment, she felt something stirring inside of her - there was a movement in her stomach, as though there was something alive just waiting to escape. As the thing emerged from the man's body, she descended into a deep blackout, subconsciously grateful that she would not witness any more of the horror.

*

She led the way through the narrow corridor and as Tyler followed he noticed the occasional door leading off on either side.

"These doors," he started, "where do they lead to?"

"To the other houses," Lana called back without turning to acknowledge his question. Their voices bounced off the stone walls.

As he contemplated her answer, he realised that they were directly beneath Cemetery Road, a chill ran through his body, *why would there be a secret tunnel beneath the street with underground access to everyone's homes?* He thought.

"This used to be a main coal mining tunnel in the early eighteenth century," She said as though detecting his question. "There were a number of smaller separate tunnels leading off from it but the tunnels were closed off after a large part caved in and killed six men, the guardians use them for access to all of their homes now."

"You know about the guardians? How do you know all this?" Tyler asked, he was growing aware that he was bombarding her with questions again.

"I did some research before I came here," she replied as she continued to lead the way.

Tyler had detected a slight American accent earlier on, "where are you from?"

"New York City," she replied, "I should tell you something first-" she stopped and turned to face Tyler, her eyes radiated grief. "Before I can show you what I am about to show you, I need you to know that I wrote the letter. The one from your sister."

Tyler screwed his face up, *why would a complete stranger write a letter pretending to be his sister?* He thought and a panic began to constrict his chest, *I was lured here,* he realised, *this is a trap, I've been lured to this strange little town where no one can find me.*

"I know how crazy this all sounds but your sister reached out to me. She wanted to get you here. I think she wanted to see you one last time."

"One last time?" Tyler whispered, the anxiety was beginning to claw at his vocal chords.

"I don't know why I felt so compelled to help but I did, I can't explain it and then I realised that there are things going on in this world that are unspeakable. They-these things, somehow discovered that she had made contact with me and set out to kill me. I guess to stop from uncovering the truth." Lana said, her voice was beginning to quiver.

"What the hell is going on?"

Lana paused and placed a finger to her lips, "I think I hear someone."

Tyler turned around to see if there was anyone approaching them, he waited a few seconds and began to hear the sound of faint footsteps in the distance.

"Quick!" She whispered, "we really haven't got much time at all."

They started to run and with each step, Tyler found himself growing more and more confused with the situation. He'd already gathered a sense that something unusual was taking place, not only with the woman who claimed to be his sister but the entire area seemed to be caught in an otherworldly atmosphere. He was directly behind Lana and they hadn't passed any more doors for the last few hundred yards or so. The appearance of the corridor began to change as they followed it farther in. The stone walls ended and the corridor narrowed considerably. It began to resemble the coal mine tunnel that Lana had spoken of previously and they slowed their pace to manoeuvre through the tunnel better, the ceiling growing lower and lower, causing them to crouch to get any farther. Tyler had never really considered himself to be claustrophobic but the fact that they were so far underground and being followed by an unknown assailant caused a fear to rise inside of him. Quite unlike anything he had experienced before. *I was going to kill myself a few days ago*, he told himself, *it can't get any worse than that.*

"We're here," Lana said as she paused in front of him, her body blocked his view of where the destination was. She took a few steps forward and Tyler saw her walk into a large clearing. The narrow tunnel led into a large open cave, the ceiling overhead was nearly three times as high as it had been in the corridor. Directly in front of them was a large arched door built in cast iron and decorated in numerous intricate designs. The door looked somewhat familiar - and then it struck him. They were directly beneath the church.

"Through here," Lana said as she began to unbolt the large door.

Tyler stood behind her, quickly glancing over his shoulder to see if their assailant would appear. He could still hear faint footsteps echoing down the tunnel which now resembled a dark hole from where he stood. The unnerving aspect of the footsteps was that he would've expected them to sound as though someone was chasing them. Yet they continued at a casual pace. Whoever it was that following them was casually walking through the tunnel towards them. Tyler shuddered, he wondered why they didn't launch into a sprint to catch up with them. He heard a loud thud and the door began to creak open.

"Try to stay calm," Lana whispered and she stepped through the doorway.

Chapter Twenty Four

And it was in that moment - as she witnessed the life depart from the mangled body, that each and every vein in her frail body suddenly became engorged with blood. The hot sticky fluid, reminiscent of some form of organic magma rushed through her arteries with such velocity, that she too, became convinced that she was destined to depart this earth in that very second. And she accepted that terrifying notion - she embraced it with open arms and exhaled with a momentary taste of peace, convinced that it was to be her final breath. Yet, adrenaline coursed through her system ascending her consciousness to a an entirely new level of anxiety. Synapses seemed to crackle and fire, while further chemicals surged through her body and her once-perfect 20/20 vision was suddenly clouded by a cascade of white flecks that resembled surgically structured snow-flakes. She had been temporarily paralysed with the realisation of what had happened. This was the moment she was sure that she was due to pass from her corporeal being and drift into the great beyond.

This was the moment that changed everything.

Life and death.

As quick as flicking a switch.

On - off.

Tara gripped the steering wheel with such force that her fingers ached and her knuckles turned white. What have I done? She thought to herself, what have I done? A few feet in front of her car lay the body -the body of a small girl. Her once golden hair had turned dark red and she lay face down. Tara felt a moment of relief wash over her. I can't see her eyes, she thought. Thank God I can't see her eyes. The relief quickly dissolved and she was suddenly plagued with guilt. The girl must have been about seven years old and Tara realised that she would never get to taste another slice of birthday cake ever again. She wanted to get out of the car and check on her. She wanted to call for help, call for an ambulance or the police but she didn't. Why would a young girl be out on her own in the evening in a desolate part of town? It's her fault, Tara thought. She shook her head to try and rid the thoughts. I need to get help, that's what I need to do. I can't just leave her here. Yet Tara found herself pressing her foot down on the accelerator and swerved to avoid hitting the body once again. She sped down the road as fast as possible, it didn't happen, she told herself. It just didn't happen.

*

There was no way for Tyler to brace himself for the sight behind the cast iron door. As his pupils dilated in an attempt to understand what it was that he was witnessing, he knew that very few people had laid their own eyes on such sights. The cavernous room seem to stretch on endlessly. Rows and rows of half-naked bodies stood upright in long aisles that stretched as far as the eye could see. Tyler was reminded of rows of crops - the way they were so orderly and neat. The only exception were the hundreds of wires that seemed to be connected to various parts of their bodies. The wires trailed at their feet and above them following a long metallic scaffolding that held their bodies in place. A strange whooshing noise could be heard all around them followed by the occasional soft beep. Tyler took a step closer to one of the rows and tentatively peered at one of the bodies. An older woman, her eyes were closed shut as if sleeping. Her arms lay limply by her side and her knees were slightly bent. He observed many of the wires entering her body at various points, the skin at the entry points looked slightly red and irritated. As he stared a little longer, he noticed her chest rise and descend slightly - she was breathing.

"They're still alive?" Tyler turned back to Lana.

She approached him and took a moment to observe the body, a look of sorrow had gripped her facial features, "yes," she replied.

"I don't understand, what's going on?" Tyler expressed.

"They're volunteers," Lana started, "they temporarily give up their bodies."

"Temporarily?"

"Tyler, your sister is one of these volunteers," Lana said abruptly as though she couldn't hold the information in any longer.

"What!?" Tyler exclaimed, he quickly scanned the bodies, "she's here? But that woman-?"

"I don't understand it fully but she's involved with something-" Lana paused.

A voice appeared behind them and finished her sentence,"Inhuman."

Tyler and Lana quickly spun around to see who it was that had uttered the word that had caused a sensation of dread to descend on Tyler like dead-weight. It was the man that Tyler had met earlier on, the man who called himself Roy.

"Get the fuck away," Lana said as she pulled out a gun from her back pocket and aimed it directly at his head.

"You weren't listening, I said inhuman," he spoke calmly with a slight grin flickering on the edges of his mouth and a spark of green emitted from his eyes. "You think a bullet is going to stop me?"

"I don't fucking care asshole, get back!" Lana shouted.

He took a step towards them and Lana fired off a round in quick succession. Dark holes appeared in his face, one beneath his eye and several in his forehead. Blood began to slowly trickle from each of the entry points, thin red lines that collected at his chin and began to drip on to the floor. Yet the same surreal grin stayed on his face as though he was enjoying his grotesque display. Tyler had been rendered silent, the shock of the whole situation was beginning to set in. He wanted to find his sister and get as far away from all this madness as quickly as possible.

"See, I said your bullets are useless," he spoke calmly still, letting each word float into the abyss of the room and deliver a punch with each syllable.

Tyler had detected an evil within this man since the moment he had first seen him but now he wanted him gone and wished he had come prepared with a weapon. He quickly scanned the room to see if there was anything he could use.

"I've killed several of you fuckers, I know you can die!" Lana screamed as she reloaded her gun.

Tyler noticed her arms were shaking.

"What have you done with my sister?" Tyler shouted.

Roy took another step towards them and Tyler witnessed the oozing red blood that streamed down his face begin to change colour. At first it seemed to darken before it appeared as a bright luminous green.

"W-w-what?" Tyler whispered.

"Ahhhhh now you're beginning to understand," Roy said in a response to Tyler's bemusement. "Inhuman." He repeated and licked at the blood that had collected around his lips.

"They somehow get people to bargain with them," Lana said as she clicked the cylinder closed and flicked the hammer back with her thumb. "People give up their bodies so that these creatures can use them."

"You've been researching us," Roy laughed.

"They use them," Lana sputtered breathlessly, "as hosts, they grow things inside of them. He-" she pointed towards Roy, "he is a guardian, he's one of many, holding the others as prisoners, making sure they don't attempt to contact anyone from outside of their community of dead-body-hogging souls-"

"That's enough!" Roy snapped and began to lunge at Lana.

She quickly fired off another round but it wasn't enough to stop him tackling her to the ground. Lana screamed as he placed his hands around her neck. In that moment, Tyler felt a burst of energy infuse his muscles and he found himself on top of Roy. He began to push his fingers under his collar and began to pull him off Lana but he found his fingers sinking into the flesh that resembled wet putty. It felt loose, like the flesh of an over-ripe apple. Tyler used all his strength to pull Roy backwards and as he threw him to the floor, he noticed his hands were covered in the red-green fluid which felt cold to the touch.

"You have no idea what you're about to do-" Roy began to shout.

Tyler stepped over and raised his foot over his face, "fuck you!" He shouted as he brought his foot down with as much force as possible. His face exploded, sending fleshy lumps of skin and muscle tissue in various directions. The strange red-green blood splashed all up Tyler's leg but he used his heel to grind away at the back of his skull. He was surprised at how easily he was able to get his foot through the bone, as though it wasn't made of collagen and Calcium Phosphate like a normal human body. It was as though he was wearing some sort of human 'skin suit'.

Lana had picked herself up and rubbed at her neck, "you really got him good huh?" She said and offered up a weak smile. "Come on, we still don't have much time." Lana flicked her head from side to side and began to run towards one of the rows of bodies, she turned up one of the aisles and shouted for Tyler to follow. He did as instructed and launched into a sprint. He found it unbelievable that such a place existed and that it had been kept secretive for so long. He watched Lana stop and stand in front of one of the bodies.

"Here!" She called to him.

Tyler continued to run towards her, his heart was racing. *I still don't understand*, he kept thinking. He stopped when he reached Lana and followed her eye-line. He sharply inhaled with shock and he was visited by that familiar sense of dread once more.

"Tara-?" He whispered weakly. She looked exactly the same as when he had last seen her. Her long brown hair cascaded down both shoulders and her petite heart-shaped face seemed untouched by age and though she looked pale, she looked peaceful - as though she was sleeping.

"She contacted me," Lana said. "Look over there," she pointed to the far end of the wall and Tyler saw a long row of old looking computer monitors. The screens rolled and flashed with various words and symbols but he was too far away to make out what any of it said. Thousands of wires branched out from behind the computers and trailed over water pipes that ran above the rows of bodies. These were the same wires that were connected to the bodies.

"She somehow managed to get online through these connections and send a message. God knows how long she was trying for and I don't know why me-" she paused "maybe I was the only one that would listen." Lana said. "She asked me to write the letter, to get you to find her here."

"So that woman? Living in that house? She knew things only my sister would know-I don't-" Tyler could feel the rush of the questions boiling over the surface.

"This is where it gets a bit fuzzy." Lana said, her eyes still fixed on Lana. "I've been living in these tunnels for a few weeks now. I've been in each of the houses and I've tried to get information from this place. I don't know what to call it - this-this farm," she took a deep breath. "That woman is also your sister."

Tyler felt his eyes peeling away from Tara's body and replaced his gaze upon Lana, "what?"

"As far as I understand it, these things. I think they're some form of demon or monster or something. They're creating a mixed breed. Half human, half whatever they are. They use the bodies to harvest the young, the birthing period lasts for years. They used to just take the bodies of people, dead or alive and try to create hosts from them but the brood never survived. That was until they realised something. A body with a soul removed provides the perfect habitat. Even though it takes years for their young to grow, they arrive healthy and they can pass as a human. Despite some tell-tale signs like a change of colour in their eyes and some other peculiarities."

Tyler could not believe what he was hearing, his brain felt compounded with all the information that he would have described as ludicrous and insane but somehow made more sense than anything else.

"I don't understand the procedure but they remove the soul of the volunteer and they allow it live a life in the body of another. A recently deceased person-"

Tyler had a flash of the moment in the restaurant where the lady had approached them and seemed in complete shock over Tara. He recalled how she had pointed her finger and cried out 'you - it's you'. He shuddered with the horrifying realisation that the woman must have been a friend or a relative of the body that Tara's soul was residing in. The shock of seeing her dead body walking around as though it was a real person had undoubtedly caused her death.

"This is too much-" Tyler said.

"I'm sorry, I know how crazy this is. I've spent every waking hour here putting all the pieces together. Researching stories online where I can, listening in to the dinner parties that they host, gathering information. The body and the soul can exist without one another, almost like splitting the person in two."

"So everyone living in this town is a soul of one of these people," Tyler pointed to the bodies hooked up to the wires, "but living in a dead body?"

"I'm sure that everyone on this street is." Lana answered, "they also have minders or guardians that keep a watchful eye on them. People like Roy. They live amongst them to make sure that they are not communicating with people they shouldn't otherwise they will lose their bargain. They gather at the dinner parties in order to keep an eye on each other, to make sure no-one is breaking the agreement. It also gives them some sort of sense of community spirit or something."

"I don't understand the bargain part?" Tyler asked.

"Have you ever done something you've deeply regretted and wished you could turn back the clock?" Lana asked as thoughts of killing Phoebe flashed through her mind.

Tyler nodded as a barrage of regrets came to him.

"Well, you agree to have your soul removed and give them your body for a certain number of years. They promise to remove your guilt forever and then return your soul to your original body as though nothing has happened. They target desperate people in desperate situations."

"So Tara will eventually get her body back?" Tyler whispered, freshly instilled with a glimmer of hope.

"Not necessarily," Lana replied, "it depends how the brood is born, I've seen bodies ripped to shreds during the birth. There's no way they can be salvaged. Not all but some. I think your sister realised that the bargain was flawed after she had agreed to do it and that was why she reached out to me. I think she just wanted to see you one last time before-"

"One last time? But we can help her, can't we? I mean she must still be alive if she's been able to reach out to you. I can see her breathing!" Tyler shouted.

Before he could allow Lana to respond, he reached up and grabbed Tara's body and began to pull her down from the rack.

"No!" Lana screamed.

Tyler fell backwards, the body of his sister landed directly on top of him. The wires that she was connected to pulled at the water pipe ahead and they heard a loud creaking noise and deafening crack as the pipe burst open. Water gushed down onto the row of bodies. Sparks flew and the smell of burning flesh began to ascend in the air.

Chapter Twenty Five

*She wore dark sunglasses and clasped a cup of hot coffee in both hands. Yet they still trembled causing tiny ripples to appear in the dark liquid. She would have guessed that it had been about a week since she had taken the life of the little girl although the days and nights had melded into one continuous stream of guilt. She hadn't gone to work. She hadn't gone to the police. She barely slept and she contemplated taking her life. But that would be too easy, she thought. I don't deserve that. She considered a life behind bars - now that would be more fitting, she considered, and though she picked up the phone on several occasions ready to report her crime - she never did. Instead, she replayed the horrifying moment her vehicle hit the little girl's body. How easy it was to extinguish her life. How she had looked like a doll - alone and broken on the road. She had wanted to cry, or at least scream at the top of her lungs but the emotions were un-tappable. This was her second murder. Years ago she had murdered her mother with her brother bearing witness to the whole event and though she had never mentioned it to him again - she knew that he was aware that she was a killer and that destroyed a part of her. She had grown accustomed to living with the guilt. She knew what it was like to have blood on her hands but this time it was different. She had taken an innocent life. She only read the newspapers once. She wanted to be sure that the event had not been some terrible nightmare and when she read that headline: **Seven year old killed in hit and run. Investigations underway.** She knew at once that there was no returning from what she had done. She didn't know what day it was when she had taken a seat in the small bistro. She occasionally held her head in* her hands, trying to make sense of everything. Moments later, Tara raised her head, her eyes glazed over while attempting to read the chalked out menu behind the counter. She couldn't face looking out of the window. She didn't want to see the world revolving despite her crime. *I used to be a good person,* she told herself. As though summoned by her words, a man sat down next to her. She didn't look at his face straight away.

"May I sit here?" He said, his voice was raspy, either a heavy smoker, drinker or both, she considered.

Tara didn't answer his question, she had hoped the dark glasses and her anguished features would not only drive away the waitress but also any offending company.

"I might be able to help." The man croaked.

"Please, just leave me alone," Tara replied, her eyes unmoving from the menu ahead.

"You don't have to say anything, just listen-"

"Look whatever it is that you're after, you're looking in the wrong place. Please, just sit somewhere else." Tara said more sternly this time.

"I know you killed that little girl."

His words entered her like a knife in butter but she held back from showing any response.

"What if I told you I could make it all better for you. Make that guilt lift away like a stain removed from a new shirt." He spoke carefully, almost rehearsed. "I have a friend, he can help you. No questions asked. I can introduce you to people who've had the treatment and can attest to how amazing it is. You can go back to living your life, you'll be free."

There was something odd about what the man was saying, as though he was beginning the patter of a magician about to perform a miraculous conjuring trick.

"We will look after you, every step of the process, and you won't be alone," he said.

Tara didn't want to hear what he was saying, she wanted him to leave but there was something unusual about the way he talked about this revolutionary process. The idea of being guilt free seemed utterly tempting. If she could let go of what she did to this little girl then maybe she would have a chance to life a normal life. She could live with what she did to her mother but this time, killing a child - It was different. But it wouldn't bring her back, she thought.

"Look, you don't have to commit to anything. Your secret is safe with me but trust me when I say that I can help you," he continued.

She heard him rustling in his pocket and then he slid a business card across the table and left it next to her coffee cup.

"Here is the number of my friend Roy. If you have any questions then contact him. You've got nothing to lose," the man said and Tara heard him rise to his feet.

Blood rushed to her head. A mixture of emotions, anger and shame seemed to boil to a crescendo and she turned to the man.

"What makes you think that you can help me?" She bellowed, unaware that the occupants of the bistro had all stopped what they were doing to observe her outburst. The man looked older than she had anticipated, his short hair was silver and his face was lined with deep-set wrinkles. He wore a long black raincoat and a fedora to match. She couldn't help but noticed that his body shape was unusual, like he was carrying extra weight that hung loosely in

several areas and he wore the raincoat purely in an attempt to disguise it. He
turned back to her and briefly removed his hat before offering a quick bow.

"Maybe I can't," he said before replacing the fedora and continuing out
of the door.

If Tara had looked hard enough, she would have noticed a green hint in
his eyes as he spoke. instead, she took the business and slipped it into her side
pocket.

*

Fragments came back to her. Like memories of dreams from years gone
by. Faded and distorted - except they weren't dreams. They were nightmares.
She remembering killing the little girl - that was the first memory. She
remembered the business card and picking up her phone, intoxicated and
desperate. She remembered moving to Edenville. The address of the idyllic
cottage and meeting Roy. Then it all became blurry - a procedure took place
and she lost part of herself. She had somehow become incomplete and she
couldn't understand why. She remembered awaking on the rack and seeing the
other bodies, the man whose body was ripped apart from something emerging
on the inside. She recalled connecting to a massive source energy - a network
of information flooded through her and it was unbearable, like endless
currents of electricity flowing through her, singeing every single nerve ending.
With this connection made to this powerful source, her mind's eye conjured
numerous images of fantastical landscapes, of unusual creatures one of which
resembled a large black butterfly. An image which gave her a strong sense of
power. She also remembered brief bouts of communication through this
source, those that she communicated with wouldn't believe her story so she

attempted different tactics. Numerous ways and means to contact her brother but she couldn't locate him directly, she needed help in doing so. She contemplated contacting the police and getting them involved but she didn't care about that now, she needed her brother and wanted to apologise to him for all the terrible mistakes she had made. For taking his mother - their mother. For distancing herself. There was so much she wanted to try and set straight, even it was just for him. She remembered the help of a psychic, someone named Orla and how she had promised to bring Tyler to her. As those memories flashed before her, a startling bright white light dissolved them and she found herself opening her eyes. There, staring directly at her, was Tyler. He was smiling and a bright aura surrounded him.

"Tye-" She whispered. "You came for me."

Tyler continued to smile at her as she began to become aware of her surroundings. The cold floor beneath her. The sound of gushing water. Sparks of light in the distance. Another face, a girl also looking down at her. She came to the realisation that she was on her back, presuming that she'd somehow come loose from the rack that had held upwards for so many years and it felt great to have finally succumbed to gravity.

"Tye, I'm so sorry," she whispered, there was not much strength left in her body but she was able to slowly raise her left arm. She clenched her fingers into a fist and hooked out her pinkie finger. She remembered feeling his wrap around hers and she was able to let go.

"Tara!" Tyler screamed. "Stay with me - please!"

Lana grabbed him by his shoulders and pulled him back.

"It's just her body Tyler," she tried to soothe him but she could feel his body begin to convulse as he sobbed.

"Tyler, we need to get out of here, this place is becoming a death trap," she urged as she noticed that more cables sparked and began to flick around like frenzied snakes. She looked around at the other bodies, some of them had also become conscious and began showing movement.

"They're waking up!" Lana shouted.

Tyler stood slowly, his eyes unmoving from Tara's body, "something's wrong," he said.

"What did you say?" Lana shouted, the sound of the water was becoming deafening as more water poured down on the ground, making a slapping noise as it connected with the cement.

Tyler began to step back from Tara's body and then she heard it. A horrifying crack as Tara's head snapped viciously to the left.

"What the-!" Tyler shouted, his eyes widened with disbelief.

The pair of them watched as Tara's neck began to move, forming a bubble of flesh the size of a tennis ball that throbbed and swelled. The veins and blood vessels became clear through the skin each time it swelled a little larger.

"Something's trying to get out of her," Lana whispered shakily.

The sound of several more similar sickening cracks could be heard from various locations around them and they saw the other bodies that had fallen from the rack begin to contort in various directions.

"Holy shit!" Tyler screamed.

His cry was drowned out by another noise, a deep booming voice was projected from the area by the entrance. It sounded like a wild animal ready to attack its prey - a deafening growl that bounced off each and every surface of the room. Lana and Tyler turned to see what had caused the noise and witnessed something at the far end of the aisle of bodies. A large dark shadow that seemed to be attached to something. Tyler squinted to try and see what it was that was approaching them and as the slow realisation hit him, a fear of unmeasurable degree seemed to implode from the marrow of his bones. He had never seen anything like it before in his life. The large dark beast of a shadow was the first thing he noticed, it seemed to be emerging from something - a body.

A headless body - it was the body of Roy.

Chapter Twenty Six

The large creature was dark in colour and shaped like an elongated human, it towered at what appeared to be eight feet tall. It shook off the remainder of Roy's body, like removing a leg from a pair or trousers and emerged fully from the human shell. This was the true face of one of the guardians and with another loud roar it began to bound down the aisle, pulverising the fallen bodies with each heavy foot fall. Another loud crack could be heard and Tyler looked down to see a hand reached out from within Tara's neck. The thing that was inside of her was also beginning to emerge. The hand was attached to a long arm that stretched out towards them as more of it began to slither out of her body. Without a second thought, Lana aimed her gun right at the newborn entity and delivered five shots to the palm as it reached for them. It fell limply by Tara's head - the bizarre sight of Tara's head twisted to the side, her ear resting directly on her shoulder and the long arm sticking out of her neck was macabre and Tyler felt a wave of nausea wash over him. He swallowed quickly to stop himself from vomiting, he couldn't believe what had happened to Tara, *it's only her body,* he told himself, *it's only her body.*

"Run!" Lana screamed as she grabbed ahold of him. Further demon creatures began to emerge from their respective hosts. Bodies snapped and twisted as demon limbs broke free from their internal prisons. They looked human-like, despite fingers that resembled claws and the occasional discolouring of the skin. They weren't fully developed yet and they were evidently seeking revenge for the disruption from their slumber. Lana fired shots at the creatures as they tried to grab at them as they charged past. Tyler could hear Roy's demon approaching behind them but he didn't want to lose his footing by casting a glance behind him. He also didn't want to see what it looked like close up. They tried to avoid the puddles that had formed from the water as much as possible, the last thing they needed was to become electrocuted bait for the demon and its newborn offspring. As they approached the far end of the wall, Tyler grabbed at the rack on the opposite side and pulled at it with all his strength. He turned to see it come crashing down knocking the demon over with a crash, a large wave of water splashed out from beneath it as it made contact with the floor. He caught a glimpse of its face; a large mouth was wide and presented long yellow teeth, sharp and jagged. Its eyes glowed green as large as saucepans. The sheer size of the demon was breathtaking and it radiated an evil unlike Tyler had ever experienced. Lana called for him and began to overturn the computer monitors, they smashed and sizzled in the water as they landed with tremendous force. Tyler caught sight of a large electricity cable and without any hesitation ran over to it and pulled it free from the wall exposing the bare uninsulated wire.

"Get outta the water!" Tyler screamed as he side-stepped onto a dry patch. Lana did as he instructed and waved to indicate she was safe. The demon roared and threw the large metallic rack to one side sending bodies flying across the cavern. Smaller demons that were half-birthed from the bodies screeched as they landed to the ground in fleshy heaps. The large guardian demon had gotten into an upright position and had started towards them again. *This is the moment,* Tyler thought as he brought the live electricity cable down to the water. A loud crack sounded moments before the wire touched the liquid and Tyler observed a small lightening bolt flash between the two elements. A tremendous pull surged through his arm and he was launched backwards against the wall as the cable began to flick back and forth in the water like an angry snake. The bodies in the nearby vicinity convulsed with the electricity and the demon appeared to freeze in position as the power surged through it. Its eyes glowed brighter and as Lana looked on in horror as Tyler lay lifeless by the wall, she feared the worst - they had just strengthened the demon. The thought hit her like a punch in the face and she fell to her knees. *Everything I've done was for nothing!* She screamed internally, she wished she had never made contact with BlackButterfly and gotten herself embroiled in this nightmare. *I've lost everything.* She was ready to call defeat, there was nothing more that could be done but as she was about to surrender - she saw Tyler begin to move.

"Tyler!" She screamed.

He pulled himself into a sitting position and rubbed his head, he appeared to be dazed.

"This way Tyler!" Lana called again. The demon roared in response and she watched as it fell face-first to the ground. The electric current was holding it back and Lana saw her opportunity to get to Tyler. She jumped and skirted around the water and managed to reach him in five successive leaps.

"We have to get outta here now!" Lana looked over to the expanding puddles behind her as they were approaching the main circuit board where all the computers had been hooked up to. "I think this place is gonna blow!"

The words seemed to spring Tyler into action, he rose to his feet and they both began to run to the other side of the cavernous room and follow another aisle down to the main entrance. Bodies continued to twitch and shake; the commotion occurring around them seemed to be waking up more of the offspring and Tyler envisioned them all exploding out of the bodies in one quick succession and lunging for them. It was this very thought that powered up his leg muscles and he sprinted, grabbing on to Lana to help her to increase her speed too. They arrived at the end of the aisle, just a few yards away from the main entrance. His heart thumped in his chest and the sound of rushing blood in his ears was deafening but he knew he couldn't stop. They were so close to escaping the chamber of horrors now. Their feet slapped against the floor as they raced towards the large cast iron door which had remained open. They charged through and Tyler grabbed the handle, the door was heavy and proved slow to close due to its sheer weight. As the gap between the door and the doorframe began to close in, he could see the large demon stirring from between the fallen racks and bodies. It roared with such force that he felt the floor and walls vibrate.

"Come on Tyler! Quick!" Lana screamed, she had already edged towards the mining tunnel.

"I'm trying!" Tyler called back.

As the door slowly moved with his body-weight he saw the demon turn around and look at him with its terrifying eyes. The green seemed to glow even brighter as though it was honing in on him. The demon began to charge towards the door and in the same moment that his fear intensified, he saw the back wall of monitors light up with a flash. The combination of flammable materials and electricity caused the entire back section to flare up and the flame-ball began to travel towards Tyler. The demon was gathering speed attempting to outrun the explosion behind it. It was merely a few feet away as Tyler felt the heat hit the door with tremendous force in the very same moment that he had managed to close it. The demon screeched from within and Tyler imagined it being consumed by the explosion. It gave him a brief moment of satisfaction but he knew he still had to get out of the tunnel. He couldn't be sure how long the door could contain the building pressure of the explosion inside.

"Keep running!" Tyler screamed towards Lana who had already begun navigating the tunnels. He followed her, throwing his weight into every step. He thought of Tara with each step, how he'd let her down. Seeing how her body had become a home to something else made him feel intensely angry. *She shouldn't have done this,* he thought as the tunnels eventually gave way to the corridor.

They closed the door behind them and Tyler looked around the basement. He now understood why the girls toys were kept down there. The soul of Tara who was living in this dead woman's body had created a shrine to remember why she was subjecting herself to the life she was living. It made sense to him now.

"I needed to hold on to the pain. To remind me why I was doing this."

The voice came from the bottom of the stairs. It was Tara, or at least the essence of Tara, now forever locked in this stranger's body. Tyler hadn't thought about the woman during the whole ordeal, he never considered that if Tara's physical body died, whether her soul would continue to live on in a dead vessel.

"Tara! " Tyler called out and ran over to the woman and wrapped his arms around the still, unfamiliar body.

Lana stood with her back to the door and smiled at the reunion.

"My body's gone hasn't it?" Tara said.

Tyler solemnly nodded.

"Don't worry, I'm still here. I felt it, when it happened. Then it all came back to me, like i had rejoined with my body again. I saw how I-I-well, my how my body reached out to bring you back to me, I had no idea. Not until now, it was like watching a dream. I saw it all. Everything. That place, that-" she stopped, "body farm- I had no idea how bad it was. Really-"

"It's okay," Tyler soothed.

"And you-" Tara looked over at Lana, "you must be Psychic Orla? You were the one that helped. You brought Tye back to me."

"Yes, well it's Lana-" Lana said, she seemed slightly embarrassed.

"I think I owe you everything." Tara said.

"No it's fine," Lana replied.

Tara walked over to her and embraced her fully, she let her go and turned back to Tyler, "I need you both to go now." She said.

"What?" Tyler asked, puzzled by her request.

"There are thousands of these body farms across the globe. This was only one. Once they find out, they'll be on a witch hunt, besides-" Tara paused and Tyler witnessed tears in her eyes. "I can't live like this."

Tyler rushed over to her and grabbed hold of her hands, "yes you can, we'll leave. All of us tonight. Lana, you and I."

"I'm sorry Tye," Tara whispered as she let go of his hands, "it doesn't work like that. I can already feel it."

"What do you mean?" Tyler questioned, a growing sense of concern was unfurling in his stomach and he began to understand what it was that she was about to say. Lana had approached them and stood by Tyler.

"Now that my body is gone, my soul is letting go. It can't last, one can't exist without the other. I can feel it. Everything's growing fainter," Tara said.

"No! I can't lose you again!" Tyler shouted sorrowfully, he began to take in large gulps of air. "I can't lose you twice!"

Lana placed an arm around him, "it's like you've lost your anchor," she said to Tara with a sad smile.

"That's it," Tara added, "I've lost my anchor, my soul has to move on now but I know it's gonna be okay. I can feel it."

"Why did you do this?" Tyler cried.

"I guess I wanted some redemption, but there was also a part of me that wanted to punish myself," she paused, "and another part of me wanted to be free."

Tyler felt hot tears rolling down his face, "I can't believe I'm losing you again," he sobbed.

"It's gonna be okay. You're not losing me, I'll visit you," she smiled, the colour was beginning to drain from her face and she began to look frail. "I'll visit you," she repeated, "keep on the look-out for a black butterfly. You'll know I'm with you."

Lana smiled at her comment, "come on Tyler, we should go."

"I can't," he said softly wiping away the tears.

Tara turned around and took a seat on the old sofa, "listen to her Tye, you should go." She began to recline back, her words growing weak, "and Lana-"

Lana looked towards her.

"Look after my little brother okay?"

"I will," she said with a smile as she wrapped an arm around Tyler's shoulders and began to lead him to the stairs.

Venice, italy

The bar terrace was bustling with energy as the sun beamed down on numerous wine glasses and dinner plates. The sound of chatter was almost musical as waiters expertly swerved in and out of tables delivering food and drinks to the lively patrons. It was early afternoon and she had ordered a large glass of the house red wine. She sat alone at the table as though awaiting a client from her escorting days. She took a few tentative sips of her drink as a man in a dark suit approached her.

"Posso sedermi qui?" He croaked as he pointed to the empty seat.

The young woman nodded as she took another sip of her drink, "parli inglese?"

"I do, I'm sorry I thought you were native, you certainly look like you belong here," he said as he offered a gentlemanly tip of his fedora before he took a seat. The sun bounced off his silver hair which sprouted out at the sides.

"My name's Esteban, thanks for meeting me here," he said as he offered out his wrinkly hand.

"Lanny," she replied.

"That's an unusual name."

"It was given to me," she started, "by a loved one."

The man nodded slowly, "do you mind if I say something?"

Lana returned the nod.

"I can tell that something is troubling you dear," he said.

"Am I that obvious?" She replied, throwing her hand to her face, as though to shade any sign of embarrassment.

"I know it's none of my business but I know why you wanted to meet today, you heard about my friend, how he can help you and there'll be no questions asked. It's a little unconventional if you will, but you can go back to living your life very soon, you'll be free of what's troubling you."

"It all sounds too good to be true" Lana exclaimed, throwing him a toothy smile which quickly changed into a frown, "but the things I've done," she started, "I don't think they can ever be fixed."

"Here's my friend's business card, give him a call. Ask as many questions as you like and you might be surprised," Esteban said.

"Is it expensive?" Lana asked.

"Oh, the cost is, shall we say, non-monetary." He grinned widely showing a set of deeply stained teeth.

"That sounds incredible," Lana said, "I will. I'll call him. Thank you."

"Be sure you do." Esteban said as he began to rise from his chair, "it was nice meeting you Lanny. I hope I'll see you again soon."

"Yes and me too," she replied and offered him another wide smile, "must be fate."

"Must be," he replied, tipping his hat as he backed away, "arrivederci!"

"Bye!"

She watched him walk away and as soon as he was out of sight, she slung back the rest of her wine and wiped her mouth with the back of her hand. She slipped the business card into her bra and picked up her handbag before walking back into the restaurant. She was relieved to escape the hot sun. Hidden away in the corner was a small table where two men sat tending to two large beers, she approached them with a smile on her face.

"We're on." Lana said as she waved for the waiter to come over.

"You sure about this?"

"Tyler, we've taken down three of these farms now. Four is my lucky number."

"Geoff, what about you?" Tyler asked as he reached over and placed his hand on top of his, "ready to do it all again?"

"How could I say no?" he laughed.

"Finish up your drinks boys, it's gonna be a very long night."

Malevolent Flesh

Drew Forest

About the Author:

Drew Forest is a UK Horror/Thriller/Paranormal author who enjoys exploring the strange and curious aspects of human nature and the haunting worlds his characters are drawn to.

From a young age, he was always fascinated with the idea of the *'monster under the bed'* or the *'thing lurking in the shadows'.* These facets of fear inspired him to find ways to investigate *'that which makes our skin crawl'.* This allowed him to give life to short tales of ghosts and monsters brought to life via his grandmother's old typewriter.

Forest has published two previous titles - his debut novel, 'The Corpse Rooms' is a story about madness and mystery. It tells the tale of Theo Randell, a man battling addiction who is forced to find the courage to face fear when everything is at stake.

For more information and updates on Forest's work, please visit the official website: drewforesthorror.wordpress.com

If you enjoyed *Malevolent Flesh*, you might also enjoy...

The Corpse Rooms - Drew Forest

"Engaging, intriguing and creepy..."
"...mixing suspense, mystery, thrills and the out right gruesome..."

Theo Randell is a good yet troubled man.

His life is thrown into turmoil when he begins to experience visitations from a horrifying entity causing him to spiral further into his past life of drink and drugs.

As Theo struggles to determine what is real and what is not, he manages to land a job at an old manor house providing him with a welcome escape from his increasingly maddening lifestyle. However, not everything is as it seems at the old Rose Maiden Manor and the mysterious owner demands that he must follow her bizarre requests. It is only a matter of time before Theo begins to suspect that the house has sinister plans for him and those he cares for.

Theo is ultimately faced with determining whether his reality is a result of his former life haunting him or if the visitations and the strange events at the manor are somehow connected. He must uncover the truth before the revelations change his world forever.

Reading the Palms of Dolls - Drew Forest

"A masterful story teller,"
"...so unlike anything I had ever read before..."

Ever since he was a young child, Jesse suffered terribly from an anxiety disorder known as Scopophobia; the fear of being looked at or being seen. He was raised by an emotionally unstable mother who kept him locked in a windowless room for the majority of his childhood due to his debilitating condition. Her only means of contact with her son was from behind a grotesque mask and at a considerable distance.

On his sixteenth birthday, Jesse eventually runs away from home and embarks on a surreal and terrifying journey that forces him to face his deepest fears and uncover some of his darkest secrets. Along the way, he meets another teen runaway who calls herself Rabbit, a tattooed, pierced, self-acclaimed 'goth' with a penchant for getting into trouble. Burdened with her own secrets, the pair become allies and are forced to work together in order to survive the bizarre and disturbing events that unfold in October 1994.

Both Novels are available on <ins>amazon.co.uk</ins> & <ins>amazon.com</ins> in both ebook and paperback format.

46483350R00148

Printed in Poland
by Amazon Fulfillment
Poland Sp. z o.o., Wrocław